ALL IS WELL

ALL IS WELL

Kristin Embry Litchman

Delacorte Press

Published by
Delacorte Press
Bantam Doubleday Dell Publishing Group, Inc.
1540 Broadway
New York, New York 10036

Library of Congress Cataloging-in-Publication Data
Litchman, Kristin Embry.
    All is well / Kristin Embry Litchman.
      p.   cm.
    Summary: In Salt Lake City in 1885, Emmy tries to maintain a friendship
with Miranda, a Gentile or non-Mormon, even though Miranda's father
works for a newspaper that says polygamists like Emmy's father should be
jailed.
    ISBN 0-385-32592-4
    [1. Mormons—Fiction. 2. Polygamy—Fiction. 3. Friendship—Fiction.
4. Salt Lake City (Utah)—Fiction.] I. Title.
PZ7.L69735A1   1998
[Fic]—dc21   97-31623
                                                                          CIP
                                                                           AC

The text of this book is set in 12-point Adobe Caslon.

Book design by Ericka L. Meltzer

Manufactured in the United States of America
June 1998
BVG   10 9 8 7 6 5 4 3 2 1

For William, for always, with love

1
NEW NEIGHBORS

Emmy Frailey saw the wagon as she pattered barefoot down the back porch steps on her way to gather eggs. She let the egg basket fall to the ground and shouted to her brothers, who were hoeing beets down by the barn.

"Ammon! Aaron! Somebody's moving into the brick house."

Now this was news! Nobody had ever lived in the spanking-new house on the corner. The boys dropped their hoes and ran after Emmy through the corn patch and apple trees. A fence of thin logs divided the Frailey property from the driveway of the new house. The three children sat along the top log and watched the activities next door.

Brother Jennsen's huge white Percherons clopped down the dusty drive, pulling a wagon full of furniture and wooden barrels. The two horses jingled to a stop when Brother Jennsen called "Whoa!" They stomped their big-as-buckets feet and tossed their heads, flinging foam from their mouths. Brother Jennsen set the brake on the wagon and climbed down to unhitch his team.

"You there!" he called. "Aaron and Ammon. I'd be thankful if you'd tie these horses in the shade by that barn trough."

The boys scrambled down off the fence and reached up to the horses' bridles. While they led the big Percherons down the drive, Brother Jennsen and his two strong sons began to untie the ropes that held down chairs, sofas, mattresses, a heavy round table, and the carved headboard for a narrow bed.

Who would sleep in that bed? Emmy wondered. Might it be a girl? Oh, let it be a girl, ten years old! There were few girls her age in her ward, the part of the city where she lived.

Ammon and Aaron climbed back up on the fence beside their sister. "Those are *some* horses," said Ammon.

Aaron nodded his head. "Big, but they're awful gentle."

"I don't see why *I* couldn't help," said Emmy, though the size of the huge animals made her insides quiver. "And don't say it's because I'm a girl. I can ride our Rust as good as you."

" 'Course you can," said Ammon. "But we're two years older'n you, see."

"And two years taller," added Aaron.

"Not much taller." But Emmy knew they spoke a truth that couldn't be changed. She pointed to the round table that the Jennsens were easing out of the wagon. "Say, did you ever see a table like that before?"

Aaron considered it for a few moments. "Pa could make one like it."

"Or better," said Ammon. Emmy nodded in agreement. They all knew that their father was the best carpenter in Salt Lake City.

The three children watched the hot work in comfort, shaded by the apple trees on the Frailey side of the fence.

"Awful lot of stuff they have," said Ammon.

"Awful lot of house for it to go into," said Aaron. "That house'd make two of yours."

Emmy turned to look at her own little adobe home and then back at the tall redbrick house. "Maybe three of ours," she said. "It's got a whole cellar underneath, not just a climb-down."

A shiny black horse pulling a shiny black buggy with red wheels came down the drive and stopped next to the wagon. "Whoa, there, Coal Dust," said a man. He jumped out and reached a hand to help a woman step down. The man looked to be taller than Pa. He wore a dark suit, a striped shirt with collar and cuffs, and a small tie, instead of a loose blue shirt and work pants like Pa's.

The woman was small and slight, with a neat little nose

and mouth. The heavy folds of her crimson dress shone in the sun. Her hair was brushed up under a feathered hat, not just twisted and pinned like Ma's and Aunt Zena's. And she wore gloves. Gloves, on this hot day! She looks like she's dressed for a ball, Emmy thought.

The woman spoke quietly to Brother Jennsen and went up the back steps into the brick house. The man drove the buggy to the big barn at the end of the drive.

Suddenly the fence shook. Sam, the youngest Frailey, was trying to haul himself up. "Emmy," he said, "Ma says . . . Oh! What's that big wagon for?"

"Somebody's moving into the new house." Emmy reached down a helping hand. "Maybe they'll have children."

"It's Gentiles moving in," Aaron told her. "Pa won't like us coming over here."

Emmy had heard about Gentiles all her life, but never had she seen any. "How do you know it's Gentiles?"

"Pa said," answered Ammon, just as Sam asked, "What's Gentiles?"

Emmy looked uncertainly at her brothers. "Gentiles? Virginia said the Gentiles chased the Saints out of Illinois so they had to come live in Utah Territory."

"All I know," said Ammon, "is that everybody who isn't a Latter-day Saint like us is a Gentile."

"Do you know any Gentiles?" she asked.

"*I* don't," said Ammon. "Do you, Aaron?"

"I think I saw some once, when my ma took Virginia and me down to the Tabernacle."

"What did they look like?" asked Emmy.

Aaron shrugged. "Oh, just like people."

"Then how did you know they were Gentiles, not Saints?"

Aaron scratched his head. "Because Ma told me they were, I guess."

Sam said, "Hello, man," and the other three children looked down.

The man from the black buggy stood by the fence. "Good morning," he said, and he tipped his hat to them.

Emmy's face grew hot. She hoped he hadn't heard any of their talk about Gentiles. Ammon and Aaron ducked their heads and stared at the grass growing along the edge of the drive. Emmy said, "Good morning." But she wasn't watching the man. She was watching the girl with him. The girl looked to be about Emmy's own age!

"We are your new neighbors, the Champions," said the man, putting his arm around the girl. "This is my daughter. Miranda, you get to know these youngsters while I go talk to the moving men."

"Who are you?" asked Miranda. Her thick smooth dark hair was tied back with ribbons that matched the pink of her gingham dress. She had no pinafore over her dress, and she wore shoes and stockings.

Emmy glanced down at her own dirt-stained pinafore and bare feet. She hooked her dusty feet behind one of the fence logs to hide them.

"My name's Sam Joseph Frailey," said Sam proudly.

"Hello, Sam Joseph. Is this your sister?"

"That's my sister Emmy. I had a birthday and now I'm four." Sam held up four fingers to make sure the girl understood.

"Are those your brothers?" asked Miranda.

"Yes," Sam told her. "That one's Ammon, that one's Aaron." The boys hung their heads. Emmy was trying to think of something to say when she heard Ma calling.

"Sam! You, Sam. What did I tell you?"

Sam looked around guiltily. "I forgot. Ma said the twins have to go hoe. And something else." He rocked gently on the top fence log while he thought. "Oh, I remember. Aunt Zena says she needs some vegetabables for her dinner."

"What kind of vegetabables?" asked Emmy, trying not to laugh. Miranda grinned at her and Emmy smiled shyly.

"She said she told Aaron already," Sam said.

"I forgot too," said Aaron. "She said beans, potatoes, corn, and tomatoes, I think. You want I should get potatoes out of the root cellar for your ma, Ammon?"

Ammon nodded. "And I'll pick the beans." Reluctantly they climbed down from the fence.

Emmy remembered manners for her family. "Say goodbye, twins."

"Goodbye," they mumbled, and ran to the garden.

"Are you a Gentile?" Sam asked Miranda. Emmy wanted to know too, but she put her hand over his mouth. Pa said the Gentiles didn't like to be called by that name.

"I'm a Champion," said Miranda, "I don't know the Gentiles."

Sam squirmed away from his sister's hand, shaking the

fence. "They're moving into the brick house," he said. "*Don't*, Emmy. You hurt."

Emmy said hurriedly, "Miranda. That's a pretty name. Are you going to live in that house?"

Miranda nodded. "Yep." She straddled the fence by Emmy and pointed to the adobe house. "Do you live over there?"

"That's our—" Emmy began, but Sam interrupted.

"Your pa drives a buggy," he said. "My pa does carpenteering."

"Papa works for the *Salt Lake Tribune*," said Miranda. But she was thinking about something else. "Say, are you some of those Mormons?"

"I'm a Mormon!" shouted Sam.

"We're Latter-day Saints. Sometimes people say Mormon," said Emmy. Everybody she knew was Mormon. This was the very first person she had ever talked to who did not belong to her church. She couldn't stop looking at Miranda.

Miranda seemed equally fascinated. She stared at Emmy and then she stared at Sam and then she stared back at Emmy again. "But where are your horns?"

"Horns? What kind of horns?" Emmy was bewildered. Sam laughed and put his fingers on either side of his head.

Miranda explained. "My friends in Chicago told me to watch out for Mormons because they have horns."

"We don't have any horns! Nobody has horns."

"Oh," said Miranda thoughtfully. "I didn't really think so. But you've got twin brothers! I'd like to have a twin."

Emmy grinned. "They're not really twins. We call them

that because they're always, always together. Ammon is two months older."

"How can you have brothers that close together?" asked Miranda, yanking at one of her ribbons. "Is one adopted?"

"No," said Emmy, "they just were born that way. Ammon is my ma's boy and Aaron is Aunt Zena's."

"But if they don't have the same mother, how can they be brothers?"

"They're both my pa's boys. We all have the same pa."

Miranda's ribbon came untied and she pulled it off her hair. "My papa says Mormons have lots of wives. Does your pa have lots of wives?"

"No," said Emmy again. Why was Miranda asking about things that everybody already knew? "He just has Ma and Aunt Zena."

"He has *two* wives?" Miranda asked.

"Of course."

Miranda kicked her foot against a fence post. "Nobody I know has any more'n just one wife in their family. My mama says it's a—a *scandal* to have more than one wife."

"What's a scandal?" Emmy wanted to know.

But Miranda didn't seem to know either. She shrugged. "Oh—you know. It's something grown-ups say when they don't like the way somebody behaves."

Emmy bristled. "My pa's a very good man. Everybody says so. He's the president of our Sunday school."

"Oh, well, then *that's* all right. Say, do you have more brothers? Do you have a sister?"

"Amongst us all, there's twelve of us."

"Twelve children! How do you fit in that little house?"

"That's Ma's house. Ma has me and Ammon and Sam, and her two big boys Gideon and Oliver. See the next house over?" she asked, pointing. "That's Aunt Zena's, and she's got Aaron and my big sister Virginia, and *her* big boys Don and Martin. The four big boys sleep out in the bunkhouse by Pa's carpentry shop."

Miranda counted on her fingers. "That's only nine."

"Aunt Zena's oldest three are married—Phoebe and Joseph and Luke. They live in their own houses. Phoebe and Joseph's got babies."

"There's only me at my house." Miranda sighed. "It must be fun with so many."

Emmy had never thought about that. "I suppose it is," she said. "You better believe there's plenty work, too. My pa says, 'When all work, there is food for all,' so he sees that we all work!"

"I wouldn't mind working," said Miranda. "Mama never lets me. . . ."

A voice called out from the brick house. "*Miranda!* Miranda!"

At the same time, Emmy heard her own ma. "Emma Leah Frailey, you go fetch those eggs right now!"

The girls climbed off the fence and looked at each other. Emmy's heart began to beat faster. Might she and this Gentile girl be friends?

"Miranda!" The voice was louder. "Come here this minute!"

"I'd better go," said Miranda. "See you." She turned and ran toward her house.

"See you," Emmy said, almost too late. She stared

through the fence at the brick house until Sam yanked on her pinafore.

"Come *on*, Emmy. Ma said to get the eggs."

Emmy turned away slowly. When would she see the Gentile girl again?

2
WHO ARE THEY?

All the while Emmy did her morning chores she thought about Miranda. What made a Gentile Miranda so different from a Mormon Emmy? Could it be her pretty clothes? Or was it having no brothers and sisters?

After she made the beds and refilled the bedroom wash pitchers, Emmy went down to the kitchen. She wanted to ask Ma about Gentiles, but Ma was busy getting dinner ready. When Ma was really busy, she wouldn't listen to questions. All she said was, "Emmy, set the table."

Emmy spread a clean cloth over the long table in the sitting room and laid knives, forks, spoons, and glasses at each place. She put a stack of plates at Pa's place.

Ma bustled about in the kitchen, mashing potatoes in the big pot, stirring gravy and creamed corn. Ammon and Sam swiped bits of pickles and biscuits when they thought Ma wasn't looking.

"Slice the tomatoes, please, Emmy," said Ma. "Ammon, stay out of those biscuits. Take Sam out to the pump and scrub the both of you."

Pa liked to have dinner at midday in the sitting room. He liked to see everyone with clean hands and faces, ready for prayer, when he and Gideon and Oliver came in from their work at the carpentry shop behind Aunt Zena's house.

Pa sat at the head of the table by the stack of plates. He was a small man with a thick mustache instead of the beard many Mormon men wore. Ma hung her apron over her chair before she sat down, cool and calm, opposite Pa.

"Sam will pray today," said Pa, and they all bowed their heads. Emmy loved Sam's prayers; he always prayed about what was on his mind.

Today he said, "Dear Heavenly Father, thank you for the chickens who make our eggs. Thank you for the dirt that makes our beans. Please bless the Gentiles to be good."

After the amens, Pa began to serve the plates. "Ellen, my dear? Potatoes? Beans?"

"Some of everything, thank you, Malachi," said Ma.

Emmy was next. Pa believed that his children should eat without fuss whatever was placed on their plates. Usually he gave Emmy a heaping plateful of food because he thought she was too thin. He insisted that she swallow every chok-

ing bite. She knew right away that work had gone well in the shop today because Pa was letting her choose.

"Daughter," he said, "I know you're not overfond of these good green beans. Would you like two or three?"

Emmy said she could manage three long beans with her corn and potatoes. Hungrily she breathed in the delicious smells of hot biscuits and rich brown gravy, but she did not taste a bite until Pa had given the boys their portions and filled his own plate. Then he raised his fork and glanced around at his family, the signal that all could begin.

For a while everybody concentrated on eating. The boys and Pa were too hungry and Emmy too busy thinking about the Gentile girl to say anything. Ma cut up Sam's biscuits and beans into small bites as she said, "Gideon, Oliver, are you going to the Mutual Improvement Association meeting at the wardhouse tonight?"

"Yes, Ma," said Gideon. "We won't stay late."

"Unless Lena Jennsen is there," said Oliver. "Then Gideon might never come home."

Emmy felt the toe of Gideon's heavy boot bump against her foot as he kicked his brother under the table. But the big boys were careful not to disturb Pa.

"Pa! Pa! There was a big wagon today!" Sam said.

"Was there now? And where was this wagon?" Pa helped himself to more beans.

"At that next house, Pa—the one that isn't Aunt Zena's. And there were horses! Big horses!"

As Emmy scattered salt over her tomatoes, she looked sideways at her father. Pa swallowed his mouthful, took a drink of water, and said to Ma, "Yes, a new family moving in. A Gentile family, Ellen. You will want to be careful."

"What's Gentile?" asked Sam, holding up his plate for more food. "Aaron says Gentile is the ones that isn't us."

Pa gave Sam two beans, a dollop of potato, and some gravy. "A Gentile is a person who doesn't belong to our church, Sam. Gentiles don't follow our way of life. They drove us from our homes in New York and Ohio, and then from Missouri and Illinois, and we came west to find a place where we could worship God in peace."

His voice got louder. "But Gentiles followed us even here. And again they threaten our freedom of worship." He rubbed his mustache with one forefinger, as he often did when he was upset. "Perhaps, Ellen, it would not be amiss to tell the children they must be careful about speaking to people they don't know. Ammon! Emmy! Sam! Do you hear me?"

"Yes, Pa," said Emmy, eyes wide.

"Boys!"

"Yes, Pa," they said together.

Pa took a deep breath to say something and Emmy held her own breath. But Ma spoke first, calm as always. "Brother Jennsen and his boys brought the new family's furnishings, Malachi. It's a pleasure to watch those Jennsens, they work so smooth and quick together. Didn't Sister Jennsen mention something the other day about needing another kitchen chair?"

Emmy blew out her breath quietly as Pa began to talk

about chairs. Ma nodded to her and she slid from her chair to clear away the dirty plates.

She set them on the kitchen table near the wooden sink and carried in the small bowls Ma liked to use for dessert when Pa was there. She went back for the bread pudding and back again for the pitcher of cream to pour over it.

Pa allowed no one to leave the table until all were finished eating. Ammon, Sam, and Emmy ate their pudding quickly and tried not to wiggle on their chairs while the grown-ups discussed the afternoon's work.

"Emmy," said Ma, "Aunt Zena and Virginia need your help this afternoon finishing shirts for the big boys."

Emmy frowned and kicked the table. She had hoped to go watch the Gentiles some more. Ma shook her head at her. Emmy sat up before Pa could scold her.

At last Pa pushed back his chair. He and the big boys went back to work and the twins headed for the garden. Sighing, Emmy stacked pudding bowls and gave Sam dirty spoons to carry out to the kitchen. She wished it was Pa's week to live next door at Aunt Zena's. Then she and Ma and the boys could eat in the kitchen without the need for all this toting of food and dishes down the hall and back again. There'd be no extra serving dishes to wash, either. She could finish quickly and go talk to the new girl.

Ma took the leftover food down the steep steps to the cool dirt-floored cellar. Emmy dumped hot water from the stove kettle into the sink and splashed soap shavings to make a lather. She washed the dishes and Ma and Sam dried.

Ma liked to say that singing made the work disappear. Today she saw that Emmy was not happy about her work, so she began a favorite hymn of the Mormons:

> Come, come, ye Saints, no toil nor labor fear;
> But with joy wend your way.
> Though hard to you this journey may appear,
> Grace shall be as your day.

Emmy scrubbed hard at the plates. Sometimes she *did* fear toil and labor. She sang with Ma on the next part of the verse:

> 'Tis better far for us to strive
> Our useless cares from us to drive;
> Do this, and joy your hearts will swell—
> All is well! All is well!

By the time they finished all four verses, the dishes were done. Ma hugged Emmy. "Thank you for helping with the sewing this afternoon. I promise you will have other chances to make friends with the little Gentile girl."

Over at Aunt Zena's, Emmy found Virginia and Aunt Zena sewing in their shady sitting room. She was bursting with news about the new neighbors, but before she could say anything Aunt Zena handed her a threaded needle.

Emmy picked up a button and poked her needle through it. Aunt Zena said, "Aaron tells us there's a Gentile family moving into the new house, named Champion. He says they've got only one child."

"A girl named Miranda, just my age!" Emmy could still hardly believe it.

"Lena Jennsen's going to be their hired girl, Ma," said Virginia. While Emmy sewed on buttons, Aunt Zena and Virginia sewed buttonholes, loop-and-pull-the-needle-through over and over, very quick and neat.

"Lena's a fine housekeeper," said Aunt Zena, threading her needle. "The Champions couldn't find a better worker. Mr. Champion works for the *Salt Lake Tribune*, I believe. You need more thread, Virginia?"

Virginia took the spool from her mother. "The *Tribune* is the Gentile newspaper, Emmy. Watch out he doesn't write a story about bad little Mormon girls." She winked at her sister to show she was joking.

"Aunt Zena, are Gentiles bad?" Emmy put down the shirt she was working on. She wanted to understand.

Aunt Zena snipped thread from the last buttonhole of the shirt she was working on. "Being a Gentile isn't bad *or* good, any more'n being a Mormon is. It's what a body chooses to do that's bad or good. I know some very fine Gentiles, as well as some that can't abide our ways and so cause us grief."

"Miranda's family wouldn't cause us grief."

"Probably not." Aunt Zena folded the shirt and laid it on a chair. "You're behind, Emmy. Catch us up."

Emmy hastily poked her needle through another button. "But Pa said—"

"Pa has reason to fear the Gentiles," interrupted Virginia, glancing at her mother. Emmy watched Aunt Zena shake her head warningly at Virginia, who changed the subject. She talked about looking for a job, now that she had finished her course at business school.

An uneasy chill trickled down Emmy's breastbone. Why did Pa have reason to fear? But she knew Aunt Zena and Virginia would say nothing more.

She set her mind to buttons.

3
INSIDE THE BRICK HOUSE

When Emmy was free at last, she ran down by the fence and found a perch on the low branch of an apple tree. Here she could watch the house next door and not be noticed. As the Jennsens unloaded heavy wooden boxes and barrels, she looked for Miranda. Maybe she was inside, helping her mother unpack. What wonderful clothes might be inside those boxes?

Before long the black buggy drove down the Champions' drive and into the barn. Miranda and her father came out, each carrying a full shopping basket. Miranda held her father's free hand, swinging it and laughing as they came up the drive.

Emmy stayed still on her branch. Chewing absently on the end of one long braid, she watched the Champions disappear into their house. Would her hair hang like Miranda's, she wondered, thick and smooth with that curve under at the ends, if she brushed it out?

She felt a hand on her knee and there was Ma, standing by the tree. "Oh, Ma! Did you see Miranda?" asked Emmy. "She is so beautiful!"

Ma smiled and patted her daughter's knee. "No more beautiful than you, dearie."

For once, Ma didn't seem in a hurry to get on with her work. She stood gazing after the Champions as if she were just as curious as Emmy.

"Are Gentile houses different inside?" asked Emmy.

"Not really," said Ma. "Everybody needs the same things—somewhere to sit and sleep and wash and eat."

"Gentile families are different, though," Emmy said. "Miranda said so this morning." She scratched off a piece of tree bark. Her next words came in a rush. "Ma, why does Mrs. Champion think it's a . . . a *scandal* for Pa to have two wives? Is Pa bad?"

Ma's eyes looked out beyond the Champions' yard, far away. At last she said, "No, Emmy, Pa is not bad. Nor are the Champions. It's just that Saints and Gentiles have different ideas about families."

"What kind of different ideas?" Emmy asked.

Ma curled an arm around her daughter's waist. "God has asked the Saints to build up a righteous generation. To follow this commandment, many of our faithful men have more than one wife. We call this plural marriage, or polygamy. We believe that we are living as God wants us to live. But Gentiles have their own churches. These churches teach that each man should have only one wife at a time. Gentiles believe that polygamy is against God's laws."

Emmy chewed on her braid as she thought about Ma's words. Your family was your family, no matter if you had one mother and one brother, like Patty Spence, or three "aunts" and fourteen sisters and eleven brothers, like Howie Anderson. Why should anybody worry about how many people are in a family?

She stared at the big brick house.

"Miranda must be lonely," she said. "No sisters, no brothers, no Aunt Zena."

"Then you must be a good friend to her," said Ma, as Sam came up with something in his hand.

"Look Ma!" said Sam. "I found a green worm."

Ma opened Sam's fat dirty little fist. "Oh, Sammy, a tomato worm! Emmy, you and the twins had best go through the tomato patch tomorrow. My lands, look at that sun! Your pa will be wanting his supper and I haven't started a thing."

In the next few days, Emmy tried to ask Ma more about Gentiles, but she could never find a good time. If Ma was sitting down, somebody else was always around. If Ma was standing up, her mind was turned to ironing or potato peeling or sweeping.

So Emmy sat in the apple tree when her chores were done. She stared at the brick house at length, trying to figure out the Gentiles for herself. As far as she could tell, the Champions were people like anybody else.

They were busy getting settled in their new house. Twice Miranda waved at Emmy from her buggy. Once Emmy saw her at an upstairs window.

She wanted to talk to Miranda again, but she didn't know how to begin.

Her chance came a few days later. After the dinner dishes were done, Ma said, "I made an extra berry pie this morning. How would you like to take it over to the Champions?"

"Oh, Ma!" said Emmy. Her heart began to tickle with fright or excitement, she couldn't tell which. "But what should I say? How should I act?"

"Why, be yourself, dearie. Just remember your manners."

"I better put on my shoes and stockings. Miranda always wears shoes."

"You're only running next door," said Ma. "Bare feet are fine." But she agreed to braid Emmy's hair afresh and helped her take off her pinafore and smooth out her dress.

Emmy didn't climb the fence this time. She carried the pie carefully up the front steps of the big house. The Champions' porch ran right across the house and disappeared around a corner. The heavy front door loomed above her and her hand shook as she reached for the brass doorknocker. What if Miranda's elegant mother opened the door and said, "Who are you, girl? What are you doing here without your shoes?"

"I'm bringing a pie from Ma," Emmy told herself. "No call to be scared." She hurriedly cleaned each dusty foot by rubbing it against the other leg and rapped the knocker before she could frighten herself back home.

It seemed like an hour before somebody opened the door. To Emmy's relief it was Lena Jennsen. "Why, Emmy!" she said. "You looking for me? I was upstairs sweeping."

Emmy's quivering insides settled down when she saw Lena's friendly and familiar face. "Ma baked a pie for the Champions," she said.

"Mrs. C. will like that," said Lena, opening the door wider. "Come on in."

Emmy peeked nervously inside. "Where . . . where is she?"

"She's out to lunch with another lady," said Lena. "But her girl's here. You met her girl Miranda yet?"

"We talked some once," murmured Emmy, setting foot at last in the brick house. Thick flowered carpet tickled her bare feet. She barely had time to look around the hall when Miranda came running down a wide curved stairway.

"Emmy!" Miranda said happily. "I wondered if you'd ever come over. Mama said I mustn't call on you until you called on me."

"Oh," said Emmy. Her tongue stuck to the top of her mouth. She stared at her bare toes on the carpet.

"Look what Emmy's brought," Lena said, taking the pie from Emmy. "You girls come on out to the kitchen and I'll give you some milk and gingersnaps."

Miranda didn't seem to notice Emmy's shyness. She took her hand and pulled her down the hall after Lena.

The Champions' square kitchen dwarfed the one at Emmy's house. In the middle of the room stood a heavy kitchen table with newspapers and writing paper scattered over it. "Clear a space, will you, Miranda?" said Lena, setting a china jar of gingersnaps on the table. "Your pa sure is a one for reading and writing whilst he eats." She took a jug of milk from the icebox, poured a glassful for each girl, smiled at them, and went back to her work upstairs.

Emmy sat on the edge of a chair, trying to sip her milk and chew her cookie politely. Half of her listened to Miranda rattle on about coming to Salt Lake City on the train. The other half looked at the kitchen. Ma would like to hear about the smooth yellow and red linoleum and the new metal sink.

Emmy heard a voice in the hall. "*Miranda.* Where are you?" Mrs. Champion came into the kitchen wearing a shiny dress with a bustle behind. A little wrinkle wiggled across her white forehead when she saw Emmy.

"Hello," she said. "I don't believe we've met."

Emmy swallowed hard. She squeaked, "Em—Emmy Frailey," just as Miranda said, "It's Emmy, Mama."

Emmy sucked in a deep breath and started again. "I'm Emma Leah Frailey from next door. Ma sent me over with a berry pie for you."

Mrs. Champion said nothing, just stood in the doorway unbuttoning her gloves.

Emmy hastily slid off her chair and stood up, afraid she had not remembered her manners. She cast about in her mind to hear what Ma and Aunt Zena said when new ladies moved into the ward. Finally she recalled. "Are you all comfortably settled now?" she asked.

Miranda's mother smiled, a tiny smile that almost immediately ran away. "Yes, thank you. And how very kind of your mother to bake us a pie. Please thank her. Miranda, I want you to meet a friend of mine who is in the parlor."

Miranda sighed and pushed back her chair. "You'll wait for me, Emmy, won't you? Please?"

"Miranda won't be long," her mother added.

Emmy promised to wait. As she turned back to her chair a gusty breeze whisked in through the open window, flapping curtains and blowing papers off the table. She rescued a newspaper from the floor and found herself holding the *Salt Lake Tribune.* The Gentile newspaper! Guiltily, looking all around to make sure nobody watched, Emmy began to read. What would Pa say, were he to know she was reading the Gentile paper?

It looked much like Pa's *Daily Herald.* Advertisements about houses and clothes and medicine for sale filled the front page. There was an article about a runaway carriage.

And then she saw the headline. "Polygamy Laws." Her heart banging, Emmy read on.

"Polygamists should be treated as the criminals they are. Fines and jail sentences await those who will not obey the laws of our country. The government is hiring deputies to see that those who break the law are brought to justice."

Pa a criminal! Pa to go to jail!

4
THE WHYS OF THINGS

The newspaper slipped through Emmy's fingers to the floor. She shivered. Blindly she stumbled out the Champions' back door. Behind her Miranda called, "Emmy, wait. Where are you going?"

But Emmy didn't answer. She wanted Ma. She could hardly climb the fence along the drive, she felt so cold even in the hot summer sun. She ran past Sam and the twins, playing under the apple trees, and through the corn patch to her house.

"Ma!" she cried, pushing open the kitchen door. "Ma!"

"I'm down-cellar, cleaning the shelves," called Ma.

Emmy tumbled down the steep steps and flung her arms around her mother. She couldn't stop shivering.

"Why, Emmy," said Ma, warming her with a tight hug. "What ever is the matter? Are you hurt?"

Finally Emmy calmed down enough to tell Ma about the Gentile newspaper. "Does it mean Pa has to go to jail?" she asked.

"There, now." Ma's gentle hand stroked Emmy's hair. "We'll try to arrange things so that he doesn't have to."

"But he might?" asked Emmy. "He might have to go?"

"I suppose he might," admitted Ma.

Emmy pulled away from Ma's hug so she could see her mother's face. "But why? Why do the Gentiles want to put him in jail? Why don't they want Pa and the others to have more than one wife?"

Ma took a deep breath and let it out again. "Those are pretty big questions, Daughter. I'll try to answer them while you help me clean shelves for this summer's canning."

"All right," said Emmy. She didn't feel so cold now.

She looked around the small cellar room, lighted by a window set in the house foundation at the top of one wall. Ma had moved the last few jars of vegetables and fruit from last summer onto clean shelves near the steps. Now Emmy helped her strip off the dusty newspapers that lined the rest of the shelves.

"We'll wash the shelves before we put fresh paper on," said Ma. "Here's a washrag. You do the low shelves and I'll do the high ones."

Emmy dipped her rag in the wash bucket and wrung it out as Ma went on. "Emmy, don't think unkindly of Gentiles. Most people—Saints or Gentiles—want to do what is right. Most want to follow God's laws. Problems come when people have different ideas about what God wants them to do."

"But our way is right, isn't it?" asked Emmy. She knelt on the hard dirt cellar floor to wash the bottom shelves.

"I believe we are following the Lord's will for us," Ma said soberly. "But I also understand the Gentile point of view, because I was a Gentile for much of my life."

Emmy stopped scrubbing to stare at her mother. "You were a *Gentile?*"

"Certainly. My folks were good churchgoing people. But they weren't Mormons. Keep washing, dearie."

"Ohhh . . . ," said Emmy, scrubbing hard. She had never thought of that before, though Ma often told stories about the New Jersey dairy farm where she grew up.

"So you see, I know about Saints and Gentiles both. Now, because the Gentiles think polygamy is wrong, Congress has made laws to stop it. And the church teaches us to obey the laws of our country."

Emmy nodded. She learned that in Sunday school.

"We must also obey the laws of God."

"Of course," said Emmy. Everybody knew *that*.

Ma rinsed out her washrag and started on another shelf. "We Saints believe that God wants us to live the law of plural marriage at this time. The government of the United States says plural marriage is illegal. We cannot obey both God and the government. What should we do?"

The choice was not easy. Emmy's rag went slowly over the dirty shelf as she thought. Finally she said, "God is

more important than the government. His laws must be more important too."

"That's what we believe," said Ma. "We Saints choose to follow God and stand up for our rights of religious freedom, which the Constitution promises us. Remember the Pilgrims, who came to this land long ago so that they could worship God according to their own beliefs? But Congress makes laws and the government must enforce them. Some of those laws say that polygamists must go to jail if they won't give up all but one wife and her children."

There it was again. Pa might have to go to jail.

"Ma . . . ," Emmy began.

"You've missed that corner shelf," said Ma, pointing. "Now, Emmy, there's no need to fuss over what hasn't happened yet."

Emmy reached her rag into the corner. "There's two more jars of tomatoes down here," she said.

"Put 'em with the others, if the tops are still all right," said Ma, moving to the next wall. She washed three shelves to every one that Emmy did. "It's mighty nice working down in this cool cellar on such a hot day."

Ma began to laugh. "My lands, I remember one day down-cellar back in New Jersey. I was sopping a wet rag over the shelves just like this."

"Tell me!" Emmy said, starting on the next row of shelves. She loved to hear stories about that long-ago time and place.

"I was well-nigh grown then, about Virginia's age. When I heard somebody come down the stairs, I thought it was my little brother Eli wanting to play in my wash water. I yelled out, 'Go away and don't bother me!'

"Well! To my surprise a deep voice said, 'I'm sorry, ma'am.' It surely wasn't Eli. I whirled around and there on the steps was the handsomest man I had ever laid eyes on. And there I was, in my oldest calico and my hair full of cobwebs." Ma chuckled again. "See if you can get that sticky spot off, Emmy. Who do you suppose it was?"

"Pa!" said Emmy, hastily scrubbing at an old spill of peach juice. "Was it Pa, Ma?"

"No, this was long before I met your pa. This fellow was tall and lean, with blue eyes and brown curls just like Gideon. He introduced himself as William Hallbury."

"Gideon and Oliver's pa!" said Emmy. Her insides tickled queerly. Ma had never talked much about her first husband.

"Of course he wasn't their pa then. That was the first time we met, but not the last. He used to tease me about those cobwebs in my hair." Ma smiled as she scrubbed. "Your rag's getting dirty."

Emmy wrung out her rag in the wash bucket and set to work again. "Why was he in your cellar?"

"Oh, he was looking for Ma, who had some chickens for sale. Eli thought Ma was in the cellar, not me."

"Did you marry him right away?" asked Emmy.

"We courted for a year or so and saved money for house goods. Then we married and settled down in a house near the school where he taught. We had our two boys and were thinking of moving to a larger community when some Mormon elders came preaching through our area."

Ma wiped off the shelf next to the one Emmy was washing. She dropped her rag into the bucket and dried her hands on her apron. "You all done? Let's rest a bit while the shelves dry."

Emmy sat on the bottom step by Ma. "Is that when you became a Mormon?" she asked.

"Soon after that," said Ma. "The words of those elders spoke true to Mr. Hallbury and me. We concluded to join with the Saints and come out to Utah Territory, though my family tried to discourage us."

"Why did your family try to discourage you?"

Ma was silent; when Emmy glanced at her she saw tears in her mother's eyes. Softly Emmy touched her hand. "Ma?"

Ma wiped her eyes with a corner of her apron. "I'm all right, dearie. I feel sad when I think about Mr. Hallbury and about my family. My parents worried partly because Utah is so far away from New Jersey. And like many other Gentiles, they didn't understand our beliefs, especially about polygamy. Of course, none of us thought then that I would one day be part of a plural marriage."

"And then Mr. Hallbury died."

"Yes," said Ma. "Mr. Hallbury caught pneumonia not long after we arrived here." She wiped her eyes again.

Emmy knew the next part of the story. "Then you met Aunt Zena at church. She was already married to Pa."

"She was," said Ma.

Emmy tugged at a braid. She found it difficult to squeeze out her next question. "Then—then why did you marry him too?"

Ma raised her eyes to the cellar ceiling as if she were looking for an answer to Emmy's question. At last she pointed to the top of one cellar wall.

"See the rows of stone, Emmy, along the top of the walls? When Pa built this house he used heavy stones and timbers to make a strong foundation. This foundation supports the walls and floors and roof of our house against wind and storm. If he'd made a shaky one, what do you suppose would happen?"

"Our house would fall down," said Emmy, staring at the big floor timbers overhead.

"Your pa," said Ma, "is the foundation of our family. He's a strong, honest man who lives up to his faith in God. Gideon and Oliver and I needed such a foundation after Mr. Hallbury died. I wanted my boys to grow up in a good home."

"Not a shaky one," said Emmy, and Ma smiled.

"When your Aunt Zena told me that Pa had been asked to take another wife," said Ma, "she said she thought I would be a good one for him. She and Pa and I talked it over and thought we could get along. So Pa and I were married. Feel those shelves, Emmy. Are they dry yet?"

Emmy hopped up to run a hand along the closest shelves. "They're almost dry. Ma, what did your family say when you married Pa?"

Ma sighed. "They worried about me, and they still do.

They also still don't agree with polygamy. But they're glad that the boys and I are cared for. I think they understand that I am content."

"But why don't they agree with polygamy?" asked Emmy, sitting down again on the step. "Why do they think it's wrong?"

Ma put an arm around Emmy's shoulders. "When I married Mr. Hallbury, the minister had us promise to forsake all others and cleave only unto each other, as long as we both should live. That is the tradition, Emmy, for the Gentiles. Through hundreds of years, people have gotten used to having only one wife.

"Yet the Bible says nothing against plural marriages. You remember your Old Testament stories. Abraham and Jacob both had more than one wife, and so did others."

"King Solomon," said Emmy. "King Solomon and King David had lots of wives."

"That's right," said Ma. "They were wealthy men, so they could take care of all those wives and children. Our own leaders will only let a man take more wives if he can care for them, and if he is strong in the faith."

One of Emmy's braids found its way into her mouth while she chewed on a new thought. "Will I marry somebody who has more than one wife?" she asked.

"I don't know," said Ma, gently pulling her daughter's braid back into place. "We'll have to wait and see. I hope you marry a faithful, loving man, whether polygamist or no. It's not easy to live the law of plural marriage. Sometimes it doesn't seem as if there's enough of your pa to go around. But then, nobody's life is easy. We've all got trials. We can choose to be unhappy or we can look our troubles in the face and rely on the Lord's help."

She tugged at Emmy's braid. "Feel better now?"

Emmy did feel better, talking with Ma almost like a grown woman. "I like it when you tell me the *whys* of things." Even as she spoke she thought of another question. "Ma, are you sorry you married Pa?"

Ma took Emmy's face in her hands so she could look right into her eyes. "Sorry, Emmy? No, I could never be sorry. Your pa is a fine man. I love him. And he's as good a pa to Gideon and Oliver as to any of his own children."

Emmy let out a little sigh.

Ma stood up and shook out her apron, ready to go back to work. Her eyes laughed at her daughter. "Think on this, Emmy: what about you and Sam and Ammon? You wouldn't even be here if I hadn't married Pa!"

5
PIONEER DAY

Emmy hoped for another chance to be a friend to Miranda. She was sorry she had run away so fast. What must the Gentile girl think of her? But for the next week she was too busy even to sit in the apple tree.

The abundant garden meant that the Fraileys wouldn't be hungry over the winter. It also meant hard work for all, preparing fruits and vegetables for drying and canning.

"My fingers are about worn away, rubbing corn kernels off the cob," Emmy grumbled to the twins.

Aaron grinned. " 'All must work so all may eat.' "

Emmy admitted that she wouldn't like to go hungry when the snow came. It was hard, though, to think about winter stews while she scraped vegetables in the hot summer kitchen.

By the twenty-fourth of July, Pioneer Day, everybody was ready for a holiday. Pa hitched Rust and Lass to the big delivery wagon. The big boys loaded jugs of water and baskets full of chicken and buttered rolls, carrots, cucumbers and pickles, peach pies, and pans of yellow cake.

Pa drove the family to Liberty Park for the ward's Pioneer Day celebration. They spread old quilts under the walnut trees near the bandstand. It looked like most of the families in the ward were there, listening to the brass band.

After lunch came the speeches. The ward bishop was first. "I'm just a young sprout," he said, and everybody laughed as he stroked his full gray beard. "But I was younger still when my family came to this valley thirty-seven years ago, in 1848. We drove our wagons through three months of frying-hot days, crackling thunderstorms, and wind that like to scoured my overalls off."

Other people had stories to tell about their own journeys across that thousand miles of wide prairie and high mountains, in the days before train tracks were laid across the country. One man's family hadn't enough money for a wagon. When he was a small boy he had ridden all the way on a handcart pulled by his older sister.

Pa talked too. "I was eighteen when I came a few years later," he said. "Salt Lake City was just getting started. I remember looking down from the mountains on log cabins, 'dobe houses, and grain fields surrounded by grass and sagebrush. I saw more mountains and the huge lake beyond.

"We came to find our refuge and our peace," Pa went on, "where we could live in faith according to our beliefs. The valley has changed. . . ."

"Changed for the worse, with all these Gentiles movin' in," growled a man with a full white beard.

One of the women said, "Watch out for your children. Some places there's stranger-men stopping the young'uns to ask about their pa."

"They want us to choose only one of our families to care for," said the first man. "What happens to the other wives and children, I want to know?"

Pa stood quiet, looking down at his family with a sadness that sent fear trickling down Emmy's front. More people spoke up. One wanted the Saints to arm and fight against the Gentiles. Others disagreed.

Emmy saw Pa's finger rubbing his mustache. Then he called loudly, "Bishop, I believe it's time for the contests."

The bishop waved his hat. "This way, this way. Over to the field. Sack races first!"

Most of the children ran ahead of him, but Emmy walked slowly behind the rest.

Sam slipped a hot sticky little hand into one of hers. "Pull me, Emmy," he pleaded, "so I can go fast enough." Emmy smiled at him and tugged him into a run.

She forgot about the Gentiles once the contests began. She jumped into third place in the girls' sack race. She and

Patty Spence tied their legs together for the three-legged race. Before they had run halfway to the finish line they crashed to the ground, but it was fun anyway.

There were foot races, a backward race, a potato-and-spoon race, hoop rolling. The boys tried to climb a greased pole. The boy who got up the farthest won a baby pig.

In other contests people tossed horseshoes, pitched hay bales, and flipped cold pancakes in cast-iron skillets. The men tried to see which of them could thread a needle and sew on a button the quickest. The women raced to hammer nails into a block of wood.

Emmy liked best to watch stick pulling. Two men sat on the ground and held a thick stick crosswise between them. The game was to see which man could pull the other to his feet.

Everybody seemed set on having a good time. After a while there were watermelons and lemonade. The grown-ups sat and talked under the trees while the children ran all over the field and along the stream, shouting, tagging, hiding.

As Emmy crouched behind a scrubby bush, she noticed Miranda and her parents walking toward the tree where the Frailey grown-ups sat talking with friends.

"Gotcha!" shouted Aaron, slapping Emmy's shoulder, but Emmy pushed his hand away.

"I'm not playing anymore," she said, and dashed past the parked buggies and wagons. But her feet slowed down when she saw Miranda's blue pleated dress, blue bows, white stockings, and shiny black shoes. She edged over to stand behind Ma to hide her mud-splashed legs and the watermelon juice on her pinafore.

Pa hadn't noticed the Champions but Aunt Zena and Ma had. They stood up and Ma held out a hand.

"Now, isn't this pleasant," she said, "to have you help us celebrate Pioneer Day. I believe you are the Champions. I'm Ellen Frailey and this is Zena Frailey. Zena, the Champions have come to live in that beautiful brick house at the end of the street. Our husband is over there, in the blue shirt."

Mrs. Champion gave a stiff little nod and clung to her husband's arm. Mr. Champion took off his hat and bowed.

"Mrs. Frailey, Mrs. Frailey, I am happy to make your acquaintances. Miss Emmy, I believe I met you the other day." He had such a friendly face that Emmy had to smile back.

Aunt Zena asked, "Mrs. Champion, how are you settling into your new home?"

Mrs. Champion, who looked like she was dressed for a fancy party instead of a picnic, took awhile to answer. "Very well, I thank you," she finally said, "though I am not satisfied with my parlor curtains. It is so hard to keep lace looking nice when street dust blows in the windows."

The women began a dull conversation about curtains. Miranda whispered to Emmy, "Where are the other children?" Shyly Emmy pointed past the buggies.

"Let's go play!" said Miranda. She didn't say anything about Emmy running away from her house. She just took Emmy's hand and pulled her toward the saplings where the other children were playing.

"What ever are they doing?" Miranda asked, her eyes wide.

At last Emmy found her voice. Here was something she knew all about. "Riding trees. You find a good one—it's got to be thin enough so's you can bend it, but it can't be too small or you'll break it. See?" Emmy pulled down a sturdy sapling, hand over hand, then wrapped her legs around it and let the tree bounce upright.

She grinned at Miranda, who grinned back and asked, "How do you get down?"

"I slide down, or you pull the tree down and try it yourself."

Miranda tried it, but her feet slipped.

"You need bare feet," Emmy told her. "Shoes aren't much good at a picnic."

"You're right," said Miranda. "My feet are awfully hot." She stripped off her shoes and stockings. The girls bounced on trees for a while and then sat on the stream bank to dangle their feet in the water.

"We never had picnics in Chicago," said Miranda. "We lived in an apartment building, away from the lake."

"This is the best picnic all summer," said Emmy.

"It took Papa awhile to convince Mama to come. Did I miss much?"

Emmy told her about the band and the races. "And of course, all the old pioneers talked," she said.

"What did they talk about?"

"Same as every year. Coming across the plains to Salt Lake Valley. They got upset this year, though, talking about the Gen—" Emmy pressed shut her lips tightly.

"Go on," said Miranda, her eyes sparkling.

"About . . . Gentiles putting Mormons in jail for polygamy," said Emmy in a rush.

"Papa told me about us being Gentiles," said Miranda, "but he doesn't put anybody in jail." She splashed her feet in the stream. "What's it like, being in your family? You know, with two wives and all."

Emmy wasn't sure what Miranda wanted to know. She tried to think what might be different. "It's more crowded, I expect, than at your house. But Ma says everybody needs the same things—food and bed and . . . and things like that."

"Well, where does your Pa live? With you or in that other house?"

"He lives in both our houses. A week in ours and a week in Aunt Zena's, turn and turn about."

Miranda thought about that. "Papa has to travel to get stories for his paper. So he's gone a lot, like your pa."

"But Pa isn't gone," said Emmy. "He's in the carpentry shop or right next door. We see him every day."

"Oh," said Miranda thoughtfully. "Then I don't see why Mama and everybody is all upset about it. The part about Mormons having so many wives, I mean."

"Most Mormon men have only one wife," Emmy said.

"They do?" asked Miranda. "Then why do some of them have more? Why does your pa have two?"

Emmy pulled a braid over her shoulder, remembering what Ma had said. "It's what God wants him to do, to build up a—a righteous generation."

"How does he know what God wants him to do?" Miranda asked.

Emmy chewed hard on her braid as she struggled to find the words to explain. "Well," she said, "Pa goes to all his church meetings and prays a lot and reads his scriptures. He says that helps him listen to God."

"I don't think God ever tells *my* papa anything," said Miranda. "Of course, Papa never goes to church, so maybe he just can't hear. Say, is that your little brother on that tree?"

Emmy looked where Miranda pointed. "Oh, no!" she cried. "The boys are bouncing Sam, and he's not big enough." She climbed out of the stream and started to run.

Miranda ran after her. Sam clung to a flexible trunk, yelling with excitement. "Bouncing me, Ammon! Bouncing me higher than the big boys!"

Even as Emmy shouted, "No, Ammon!" it was too late. Her brother pulled the tree down and let it go.

Time slowed, thickened, as Sam flew off the tree and landed in a crumpled heap on the hard dirt below.

Ammon crouched by his little brother, who didn't move. "Wake up, Sam! I didn't mean to hurt you. Sister, I didn't mean to hurt him."

"I know," said Emmy. She looked around the silent ring of watching children; at Miranda white and staring; at Ammon, choking with sobs, his face smeared with tears. "Ammon!" she ordered. "Go get Pa."

For a moment she thought Ammon hadn't heard. Then he stumbled up and ran, pushing against the earth with his bare feet as if he wanted to leap into the air and fly for help.

Time stretched once more, until Pa and the big boys came hurrying across the long grass.

Pa felt Sam all over. "Nothing's broke that I can tell. Don, Martin, Gideon, Oliver, let us lay our hands on your brother."

He and the big boys knelt by Sam. Many times had Emmy seen Pa's hands placed on somebody's head to give blessings of comfort and health. She had felt those hands on her own head when she had the measles.

Pa bowed his head. "Heavenly Father, we need your help for one of your children this evening."

Miranda slipped her hand into Emmy's and whispered, "What are they doing?"

"They are giving Sam a blessing to make him well."

"Will he be all right?"

"Yes," said Emmy, hoping that he would. Pa said that blessings worked according to the will of the Lord, not the will of human beings. She squeezed her eyes shut, praying that the Lord wanted Sam to be all right.

Pa carried the unconscious boy over to the walnut trees and laid him on a quilt. "He'll be fine," he told everybody. "We'll just let him rest."

The sun slipped behind the trees, and Miranda's parents decided to go home. "I'll be at the fence tomorrow after dinner," Miranda whispered to Emmy as she and her family walked toward their buggy.

But the Pioneer Day celebration wasn't over. And just as Ma was saying, "Perhaps we'd better take Sam home," Sam rolled over and struggled to sit up. "Pa!" he said. "Ammon bounced me on a big tree!"

"I know, Son. You fell out. Lie down, now."

Sam didn't want to lie down. "Where's the picnic?" he asked. "I want the picnic."

Finally he agreed to sit quietly on Ma's lap while everybody ate supper. Then some of the men built a fire, a reminder of pioneer campfires. Everyone gathered around. People began to sing.

Emmy liked this part of Pioneer Day best of all. They sang all kinds of songs, silly and sad, old and new: "Goober Peas," "Buffalo Gals," "Silver Threads Among the Gold," "Grandfather's Clock." Then came hymns: "O God, Our Help in Ages Past" and "The Lord Is My Shepherd." Everybody sang the last song, which the pioneers had sung on their way across the Plains. It was the hymn Emmy often sang with Ma.

> We'll find the place which God for us prepared,
> Far away in the West,
> Where none shall come to hurt or make afraid;
> There the Saints will be blessed.

Emmy stopped singing. What about Pa and the others having to go to jail or into hiding? Her throat felt tight and hot as the song continued.

> We'll make the air with music ring,
> Shout praises to our God and King;
> Above the rest these words we'll tell—
> All is well! All is well!

How could they sound so happy? Emmy wondered, when, here in the West, Saints were being hurt and made afraid.

On the way home she rode standing up behind Pa, clinging to the back of the wagon seat. She had to ask him something. "Is all well, Pa? Like the hymn?"

Pa thought for a while before he answered. "All is well, Daughter, so long as we do our duty. We have our trials and hard times, but the Lord knows what is best for us. We abide in our faith in the Lord."

Faith and trials. Ma had said much the same. Still, a little tremor shivered through Emmy as the wagon jounced home.

6
SAM'S FRIENDS

Sam had only a fat bump above his right ear from his fall. For several days Ma kept him close to her, though he protested. "The twins need my helpings in the garden."

The day after the picnic, Emmy finished her dinner dishes quickly and went down to the log fence. Miranda was waiting for her, just as she had promised. And so their friendship began.

Some afternoons Emmy found a few minutes to run over to Miranda's house. Sometimes Miranda came to make beds and clean lamps with Emmy. She liked doing such things. "Nobody lets me at home," she said.

They talked about all kinds of things—dresses and school and Miranda's old home in Chicago. They talked about Sam and the funny things he said. Together they read the stories in Emmy's *Juvenile Instructor* magazines.

After Pioneer Day, Pa went down to the wardhouse almost every evening. When he came home, he and Ma and Aunt Zena talked for hours in the sitting room or over at Aunt Zena's house. "If a stranger tries to talk to you, come right home and tell me," he warned his children.

The twins always seemed to know what their parents were talking about.

"Pa might go underground, they said last night," said Aaron one morning as he and Ammon and Emmy weeded in the potato patch.

"Underground!" said Emmy. "Is he going to live in our cellar?"

Aaron shrugged. "Dunno. Maybe. Howie Anderson's pa is gone. He's hiding somewhere so the deputies won't find him."

"Who are the deputies?" asked Emmy.

Ammon said, "There's some men get paid to find polygamists like our pa and send them to jail."

"Those deputies might get Pa if he doesn't go away," Aaron added.

Emmy shivered. "Where will he go?" she asked. But the twins hadn't heard anything about that.

The weather stayed hot, making everybody feel even more worried and cross. The children kept cool by splashing in the ditch that ran down their side of the street.

Water for irrigating gardens came down the ditches from a mountain stream.

When it was the Fraileys' turn to water their gardens a few days later, Ma said Sam could go wading with Emmy. "Mind you keep your eye on him," she told her daughter. She watched from the front steps for a few minutes before going back to her ironing.

"Here it comes!" shouted Sam, as the cool water tumbled down the ditch toward them. The twins lifted the wooden gate to let water into the Frailey ditches. Emmy and the twins had spent the morning clearing weeds out of those small ditches so water could run free into the gardens and orchard.

Now she held up her dress and pinafore, kicking her feet with each step as she waded down the street with Sam. They saw Miranda sitting on the steps of her wide front porch. Emmy waved. "Come wade with us!"

"All right!" called Miranda. She pulled her shoes and stockings off and ran down to the ditch. She stomped and splashed in the water with the others. Soon her pink checked dress was soaked. "What will your ma say?" asked Emmy.

Miranda shrugged. "It's only water. It'll dry."

"Let's walk the other way," said Emmy. "It's more fun when the water's coming toward us."

The water came almost to Sam's knees. The girls let him go first so they could keep an eye on him. Whenever they came to a flat wooden bridge across the ditch, they had to climb out of the ditch to get past it.

In the middle of the next block Miranda stopped by a

large two-story building with steps going up to a small porch. "What's that?" she asked

"That's our wardhouse," said Emmy. "We go to church there, and school. Are you going to come to our school?"

"Mama wants me to go to a private one," said Miranda. "But Papa says I'll learn more about getting along with different people if I go to the ward school. Papa usually has his way."

They squished their toes in the ditch mud as they talked. Suddenly Emmy remembered her responsibility. "Where's Sam?"

Miranda pointed farther along the ditch. "Down there, by that old buggy."

Now Emmy saw Sam, standing on the side of the street, talking to two men. She shivered. She climbed out of the ditch, shouting "Sam!" as she raced up the dusty street.

When the men saw her coming they hurriedly stepped up into their shabby buggy. One of them looked back at Emmy as their horse trotted away. He had a round face and a bushy beard. Emmy had never seen him before.

"Sam!" she gasped. "Pa told us no talking to strangers!"

"It's all right, Emmy. They said they're my friends. They said, 'What's your pa's name? Where does he live?' "

"What did you tell them?" Emmy was so upset she shook Sam's arm.

Sam pulled his arm away. "I said this week he lives at Aunt Zena's house."

Fear flooded through Emmy. "Come on, Sam," she said. "We need to find Pa."

Sam pulled at her hand. "But I didn't do all my wading yet."

Miranda hobbled toward them on her tender feet. "Emmy, what's wrong?"

"Those men want to hurt my pa. Sam, come *on!*"

Miranda ran alongside them. "What happened?"

"I think those men want to put my pa in jail," Emmy panted.

Miranda took Sam's hand. "I'll bring him back along the ditch," she said. "You run ahead to your pa."

Ma came out of the house when she heard Emmy calling.

"Is Sam hurt again, Emmy? Is he all right?"

Emmy had scarcely any breath left from her long run. "Strangers, Ma, asking Sam where our pa lives."

Ma was down the steps in a moment, looking up and down the street. "Where are they?"

"They drove away when I came."

"Quick!" said Ma. "Fetch Pa and the big boys. Tell them we need a family council over at Zena's."

Soon everyone but the twins, who were still watering the garden, gathered in Aunt Zena's sitting room. Miranda went home after making Emmy promise to tell her what happened.

Pa asked Sam to tell his story. Sam stood by Pa's knee and told him about the men who had said they were his friends.

"Did you tell them my name or show them our houses?" asked Pa.

"No," said Sam. "Emmy came then." He wasn't crying but his eyes were big and frightened.

Pa put an arm around him. "It's all right, Son. You did not do anything bad. Emma Leah, I want you young'uns to wait in the kitchen while we talk. When we decide what to do, we'll call you in again."

"Yes, Pa," whispered Emmy.

It was an endless wait. Sam kept fussing. He wanted Ma; he wanted Pa. To keep him quiet, Emmy found Aaron's slate and some chalk. Sam knelt up on a kitchen chair and she showed him how to make *S* for Sam and *E* for Emmy.

Sam liked the letters but what he really liked was drawing spiders. He took the chalk from Emmy and made a round O. He added lots of lines all the way around to make spider legs. He drew spiders all over the slate.

When Sam got tired of spiders, Emmy sang all the songs she could think of. She sang good and loud to drown out the terror in her heart.

After a while the twins came in, muddy and hungry and wondering where everybody was. Emmy told them what had happened. "I'm not sure who the men were," she said, "but they were bad, I think."

"Deputies," said Aaron. Ammon nodded.

Emmy couldn't bear to think of Pa in jail. She had to find something to do to hide such thoughts. "Help me get supper," she said. "We might as well eat while we wait."

Just as they finished their bowls of bread and milk with a sprinkle of sugar, Virginia came into the kitchen. "Pa says to come in now."

The four younger children stood in a clump by the sitting room door. Pa reached out a hand to them. "Our lives will change," he said, "and it's only right that we tell you as much as we can, for much will depend on you."

Emmy looked at Pa and Ma, at Aunt Zena and the big boys. All looked sober. Virginia wiped tears from her eyes with the back of her hand.

Pa choked over his words as if he had a lump in his throat like Emmy's. "Somebody tell them," he said, shoving back his chair. He got up and began to pace about the sitting room.

"We think that the two men who talked to Sam are looking for Pa," said Aunt Zena.

"What will happen if they find him?" Aaron asked.

"He will have to renounce part of his family or be arrested," said Virginia.

Sam looked around at the serious faces. "I don't know those words," he said.

"*Renounce* means that Pa would have to say some of us don't belong in his family," Gideon told him. "*Arrest* means the Gentiles take Pa away from us and put him in prison."

Sam began to cry. Emmy knelt down and put her arms around him. Her own throat ached with wanting to cry.

"Pa's not going to be arrested and he won't renounce any of us," Ma said. "Sam, your pa will go to live somewhere else for a while."

"He'll go on the underground," Oliver said.

Pa explained. "It means I'll live in hiding. I might have to move from one place to another."

Sam was still crying. "Where are you going, Pa?"

The grown-ups looked at each other. Finally Martin said, "Only our mothers will know, Sam."

Aunt Zena said, "We won't tell you where Pa is because we want all of you to be able to say you don't know, should anybody ask."

Pa sat down again in his big chair at the head of the table. His eyes were shiny from tears and his mustache trembled at the corners as he tried to smile. "I thank the Lord for my fine family."

Aunt Zena put a hand on his shoulder. "We shall manage, Malachi. With the help of the Lord, we Saints have always proved stronger than those who would harm us."

Pa cleared his throat. "Yes. But each must do his part if all are to survive. Don, Martin, Gideon, Oliver, pay heed."

"Yes, Pa," the big boys said together.

"You will carry on with the carpentry business. Work diligently and treat each customer fairly. Do not contract for work you are not able to do."

"Yes, Pa."

"All of you hold fast to the faith we cherish. Do not neglect your scriptures and your prayers."

This time everybody said, "Yes, Pa."

Pa went on. "We've had a bountiful garden this summer, yet I don't believe we've paid our tithes to the church. I count on you older boys to get that done."

"Yes, Pa."

"A final warning." Pa's face became stern. "Beware of Gentiles. Do not allow any in our homes."

"No Gentiles? What about Miranda?" cried Emmy.

"Miranda's father works for the newspaper that is against our people, Daughter."

"But Pa . . ."

Ma put her hand gently over Emmy's mouth. Emmy's fears and sadness overflowed in silent tears.

Pa asked Don to read Psalm 125 from the Bible. "They that trust in the Lord shall be as mount Zion, which abideth for ever . . ."

"Remember those words," Pa told his family. "When we have done all we can, the Lord will always help. Let us kneel in prayer together one last time."

He asked Aunt Zena to say the evening prayer. When she had finished, Pa said, "I feel to give each of you a blessing before I go."

He laid his hands on the head of each family member in turn, from Aunt Zena down to little Sam. To each he gave a blessing of health and comfort, of strength and protection.

When Emmy's turn came, she felt the warm weight of Pa's hands on her head. Pa blessed her to be a faithful daughter to Ma, and then he hesitated for a long time. At last he said, "Emma Leah, I bless you also to be a faithful friend."

In the morning, Pa was gone.

7
ON THE PORCH

Now there was no Pa in the shop to give Emmy the curls of fresh wood shavings she loved to smell. There was no Pa to lead family prayers or give her a good-night kiss. Sam didn't run back and forth on Sunday afternoons, fetching Pa's razor and clean shirts from one house to the other. Emmy even missed sitting-room noonday dinners. Ma and her children always ate in the kitchen now.

Some things stayed the same. Vegetables and fruits kept ripening. Ma and Aunt Zena kept bottling. Emmy kept washing and snapping, cutting and shelling. Eggs still had to be gathered, cows still had to be milked.

Emmy didn't know how to talk to Miranda since Pa's warning about Gentiles. She kept herself too busy to talk to her friend. But a week after Pa left, Miranda ran after her as she walked down the street.

"Where're you going?" asked Miranda.

"To Primary at the wardhouse."

"Is that school? Can I come?"

Emmy didn't know how to answer either question. She said, "We learn things, but it's not school. We hear scripture stories, and we sing and dance. Today we're making tissue-paper lamp shades."

Miranda's eyes lost their sparkle. "If there's scripture, then it's church and Mama won't let me go. But I could come over tomorrow and help make beds."

Emmy scuffled her feet in the dust of the footpath. But she had to let Miranda know. "My pa said no Gentiles can come into our house," she said reluctantly.

Miranda stood still and stiff. "Why did he say that?"

"Your father's newspaper says that men with more than one wife should go to jail. Pa had to go away and hide."

Miranda stared at Emmy. Then she turned and ran.

"Miranda!" called Emmy. "We can still be friends. . . ."

But Miranda ran into her house and slammed the door.

Evidently other parents felt the same as Pa. Emmy never saw any children at Miranda's house. She hurt inside for her friend, but Miranda would not talk to her even when she went down to the fence.

"It isn't fair," Emmy told Ma. "Miranda hasn't done anything."

Ma tucked a loose lock of hair back into Emmy's braid. "I know, dearie. But remember the blessing Pa gave you. You will find a way to be a faithful friend."

After the work of the hot August days, the Fraileys liked to spend the evenings on Aunt Zena's wide front porch. Sometimes other people from the ward stopped by to talk. Friends of Virginia and the big boys came to sing while Virginia played the guitar.

The women always had baskets of mending—holey socks, buttonless shirts, worn trouser knees, torn dresses. Some brought fancy work—tatting and embroidery. Sometimes Emmy sat on the steps and listened to the chatter of the women as they stitched. Sometimes she ran off with the neighborhood boys to play Duck Duck Goose or Run Sheep. She missed Miranda.

Toward the end of August came a day when heat hung in thick folds like the heavy curtains in Miranda's parlor. Emmy and Ma spent the day in the cool cellar, putting all the summer's bottled food in order.

After supper Ma took her work basket and a pitcher of buttermilk over to Aunt Zena's. Emmy followed with a bowl of sugar cookies. Sam and the twins went with the big boys to Liberty Park to play baseball.

"Though I don't know how they can, in this heat," said Virginia. She sat on the porch steps, trying chords on her guitar for a new song called "Clementine." Emmy sat by her, half listening to Ma and Aunt Zena talk about a neighbor who had moved his family to the Latter-day Saint colony in Mexico, where United States law did not reach.

Emmy wanted Pa to come home, but from their talk it

sounded as if he could not. She decided not to listen any-more. She went to sit by Virginia on the steps. "Do you think I could learn to play a guitar?"

"Let me see your hand," said Virginia. They pressed their hands together, palm to palm. "It's not much smaller than mine. I think you could play."

Emmy held the guitar and Virginia showed her where to place her fingers on the frets. She strummed her fingers across the strings. It sounded nice.

"Good!" said Virginia. "Try again."

As Emmy strummed, she heard a soft whisper. "Emmy . . ."

She glanced around the yard. Miranda was crouched down by the porch steps.

"Miranda!" Emmy's smile almost stretched her face out of shape. She handed the guitar back to Virginia, who smiled at Miranda too.

"I'm not coming in your house," Miranda said. "I'll just be here in the yard, but oh! it's so dull and lonely by myself. Could I . . . could I just sit here and listen?"

Ma heard her. "Why don't you come up on the porch, Miranda?"

Miranda hesitated. "What about Mr. . . . Brother . . . Frailey? Won't he be mad?"

Aunt Zena said, "Brother Frailey is away just now. If he were here, I'm sure he would want you to join us."

"Miranda . . ." They all heard a call.

"It's Mama," said Miranda. "I shouldn't leave her alone. She gets afraid sometimes when Papa is working late at the paper."

"It's not so very late," said Ma. "Would your mother like to come over and enjoy this cool part of the day with us?"

Miranda beamed. "I'll ask her," she said. Her white petticoats flashed as she raced home.

In a few minutes she was back, pulling at her mother's hand. Mrs. Champion hesitated at the foot of the stairs, but Ma and Aunt Zena urged her to come up and sit in the rocker.

Finally she did. "I thank you, Mrs. Frailey," she said, nodding to Ma. "And . . . Mrs. Frailey?"

Aunt Zena and Ma smiled. "Zena and Ellen," said Zena. "We're right glad to see you again."

"Emmy, pour our guests some buttermilk." Ma fanned herself with her apron. "My, but it's hot, isn't it? Usually it cools off when the sun begins to go down."

Mrs. Champion settled more comfortably into the rocker. "This is nothing to the East. Out there, it is not only hot, but damp. Seems like a body never can get dried out. Here, at least, we can hang out the sheets and know they'll be dry before night."

Miranda and Emmy had no interest in laundry. Miranda wanted to hear about Emmy's pa being gone. Her papa had explained to her the disagreement between Saints and Gentiles. "But Papa doesn't write bad things about Mormons," she said. "He writes about fires and train wrecks and famous people that come to Salt Lake City."

"Next to my pa, I think yours is the nicest one I know," said Emmy.

"He goes away a lot," said Miranda. "He says you don't

ever know when a story for the paper will come along. He's at home more than he was in Chicago, though."

"Do you miss Chicago?" asked Emmy.

"I miss my friends, but Salt Lake City is much more exciting. You have chickens and horses and cows and ditches and apple trees. There's no end of things to do."

By and by, the sky grew dark. The boys came back and Ammon took Sam home to bed. Mrs. Champion pulled herself from the rocking chair. "It's nearly bedtime, Miranda. You can see your friend tomorrow. Mrs. Frailey . . . Ellen, Zena, I'd like it fine if you could come take tea with me some afternoon."

The two women glanced at each other and smiled. Aunt Zena spoke for them both. "We'd like to do that, Mrs. Champion, if we could prevail on you for lemonade instead."

"Oh . . ." Mrs. Champion was flustered. "That's right. Mr. Champion mentioned that you . . . that the people of the Mormon faith do not drink tea. No tea or coffee, I believe?"

"And no alcoholic drinks," added Emmy.

"No alcohol. You know," said Mrs. Champion, stopping on her way down the steps, "I do believe that is wise."

Miranda grinned and whispered to Emmy, "Mama *detests* alcohol. She'll be their friend for life now."

She squeezed Emmy's hand before she ran after her mother. Warm joy spread through Emmy. Maybe I have a friend for life too, she thought.

8
GOING DOWNTOWN

"Martin's going down to the tithing office," Virginia said one September
morning, coming into Ma's kitchen. "I'm
going with him to apply for a job at the
Z.C.M.I. Do you need anything downtown,
Aunt Ellen?"

"Oh, mercy, let me think," said Ma.
"White stockings, Virginia; you know my
size. Emmy needs a new school dress, she's
shooting up so fast. Could she go along with
you and choose some dress goods?"

"She can if she'll wait quietly while I talk
to somebody about that job."

Emmy tipped over her chair in her hurry
to get up. "Can Miranda come? She can
wait with me."

Ma looked toward Martin, now standing in the doorway. "Will you have room in the wagon?" she asked.

"I'll take 'em if they're ready to go when I am," said Martin. "No lollygagging, mind. When I'm loaded, I'm leaving."

Mrs. Champion agreed to let Miranda go. She insisted on tying fresh ribbons in her hair. Then Ma insisted that Emmy put on shoes and stockings. "And take off your pinafore!" said Ma. "Is your dress clean?" It was.

At last the two girls ran down to the barn where the wagon waited. Martin was just helping Virginia up to the driver's seat. Gideon and Oliver boosted Emmy and Miranda into the back of the wagon. They squeezed between a basket of apples and another of potatoes. Eight kitchen chairs and more bushels of vegetables and fruit filled the wagon.

"Gee' up, Rust, Lass," said Don and the wagon bumped out of the drive, crossed the planks over the ditch, and turned north.

"My!" said Miranda, looking at the crowded wagon. "Where's your brother taking all of this?"

"Down to the tithing office."

"Is that a marketplace?"

Virginia heard Miranda's question. "In a way it is. Because the Lord has given us all that we have, we return one-tenth of it back to him."

Miranda was astonished. "What's God going to do with a bushel of potatoes?"

Martin grinned at her over his shoulder and then turned around to make sure the horses were going straight.

Emmy knew the answer to this question. "Maybe God doesn't need the potatoes to eat, but there are lots of people who don't have any. The food goes to poor people. That's doing God's work."

"But what about the chairs?"

Martin turned his head again. "Poor people need chairs, same's you and me. We give one chair in ten that we make."

Downtown wasn't far away. Soon Rust and Lass pulled the wagon through the gates of the high stone wall that surrounded the tithing office yard. "Ho!" said Martin, and the horses stopped.

The girls climbed down while Martin began to unload. "I'm going home around noon. You want to ride back?" he asked Virginia.

"We have our dinner with us," said Virginia, swinging the shopping basket to show him. "We'll walk home."

She wasn't in too much of a hurry to let the girls explore the yard. Wagons and buggies drove in and out. Some brought food and goods in, and some carried food and goods out. A blacksmith pared a horse's hoof. Martin waved as he left with the empty wagon. "See you at suppertime."

The huge church-owned Z.C.M.I. department store was across the street from the tithing yard. "Watch out," called Virginia, grabbing her sister's arm as Emmy walked into the street without looking. "South Temple is a very busy street!"

And it was. Emmy didn't see how they would get across. A wagon with barrels piled four high was pulled by a four-horse team, then came two fast buggies and a wagon with a family as big as Emmy's. Mule-pulled trolley cars clattered along their tracks in both directions.

Such traffic was nothing to Miranda, who was used to Chicago's crowded streets. She yanked Emmy across South Temple between two men on horseback and an eastbound trolley car. Virginia hurried after them, holding her long skirt up to keep it out of the dirt.

"Salt Lake streets are *some* wide!" said Miranda when they were safe on the other side.

"The pioneers made them wide on purpose," said Virginia. "It's very convenient nowadays. The trolley tracks run down the middle of the streets, and there's still plenty of room for wagons."

Emmy loved Z.C.M.I. It had everything anybody could possibly want: kitchen stoves, pans, fur muffs, buttoned boots, rag rugs, spool-end beds, wooden kitchen chairs and padded parlor chairs, warm flannel for winter nightgowns, bright calicos for school dresses, glass-chimneyed lamps, underdrawers, petticoats, knives and forks, baby buggies.

The manager told Virginia he could see her in an hour. "So we might as well get our shopping done first," Virginia said. "I'll find Aunt Ellen's stockings and the things Ma wanted while you girls choose Emmy's dress goods."

"All right," said Emmy and Miranda together. They wandered around the store for a while, playing the "I want" game. Emmy chose a Sunday silk dress, paisley shawl, and lace mitts. Miranda said she had all the clothes she'd ever, ever need. She chose books and a long buggy whip.

Virginia, her basket full of string-tied packages wrapped in brown paper, found them in the dry goods department.

She paid for the cloth Emmy had chosen, a dark green calico with tiny yellow flowers. "Now you girls go outside for your dinner," she said. "I'm too nervous about my job interview to eat."

Miranda bought some saltwater taffy and peppermint sticks at the candy counter. Outside she and Emmy took turns drinking cool fresh water from the dipper in one of the fountains on Main Street. There was a place for horses to drink, too.

The girls sat on the step outside Z.C.M.I. and watched buggies and wagons drive up to the big store while they munched bread and cheese and peppermint.

Women and children climbed out and went inside. Some men waited in their wagons. Others tied up their horses and walked down the street on their own business.

"There's the newspaper office where Papa works," said Miranda, pointing across the street. But they didn't see him anywhere.

When Virginia came looking for them, she still hadn't talked to anybody about a job. "It's going to take a long while," said Virginia. She kept patting her hair, fussing with the bow at her neck, shaking dust off her skirt.

"Can we go watch the templeabuilding while we wait for you?" asked Emmy.

"All right," said Virginia. "I'll come get you when I'm through."

"What temple?" Miranda asked.

Emmy pointed catty-corner across from Z.C.M.I. Above the high walls around Temple Block, a wooden cage of scaffolding surrounded a tall gray building.

This time the girls had to cross two wide busy streets. When at last they were safe outside the Temple Block wall, Miranda said, "That traffic's almost as bad as in Chicago."

"Pa says . . ." Emmy had to swallow hard, because thinking about Pa made her miss him so. "Pa says this is the busiest two streets in the West. Everything in Salt Lake City starts from here."

Inside its walls Temple Block looked almost as lively as the tithing office yard. Orderly stacks of granite blocks lay in rows. Men banged at chisels to shape the gray stones. Other men hammered on the wooden scaffolding, which made a safe working place for the stone masons. The girls held their breath as a heavy stone was hoisted up, up to the top of the scaffolding, and swung into position.

"When did they start building this temple?" asked Miranda.

"About 30 years ago, Pa said," answered Emmy, "and it's like to take years more to finish."

But something else had attracted Miranda's attention. "What's *that*?" she asked, pointing to a nearby building that looked like a long gray bowl upturned over short walls.

"That's the Tabernacle, where they hold all the big church meetings," Emmy said.

"Let's go inside," said Miranda.

The Tabernacle doors were open. The girls sat on a wooden pew and stared up at the high curved ceiling. Far down at the other end of the building a man was practicing the organ, playing the same short piece of tune over and over like Virginia did on her guitar. They counted the organ pipes while they waited for Virginia.

"What happened about your job?" whispered Emmy when her sister finally sat down beside them.

"I think it's all right," Virginia whispered back. "One of the clerks is going to be married in a few weeks. I can take her place. My, it feels good to sit down."

They let Virginia sit for a few minutes before they took her outside to show her the rock-hoisting machinery. Emmy stared at a short man standing with a group of men looking up at the scaffolding. The man had a ruffle of beard, but he stood with his thumbs hooked into his front pockets the way Pa stood, and he wore a hat that looked like Pa's.

"Pa! Oh, Pa!" Emmy started to run toward the group of men, but Virginia grabbed her arm.

"Emmy. Stop."

The man had turned toward them when he heard Emmy's voice. She saw his forefinger go up to rub his mustache. Then he turned and walked quickly away.

Now she was sure it was Pa. "Let me go!" she said. "I want to go see Pa."

"No!" Virginia spoke sharply and glanced quickly all around. "Emmy, you didn't see Pa. Now stop this and come along home."

None of them spoke as they crossed South Temple again. Virginia carried the shopping basket. Emmy dragged her feet, which ached inside her shoes. Even Miranda looked weary.

"We could take a trolley car home," said Miranda.

"I don't know . . . ," said Virginia uncertainly. Emmy knew Virginia had never ridden on the trolley cars. She didn't know any more than Emmy about how to stop a car or how to pay for a ride.

Miranda managed it all for them. She held up her hand to stop the next trolley and asked the driver, "Where is this car going?"

"Where d'you want to go?" asked the man.

"Sixth East," said Virginia.

"I'll get there eventually. Climb aboard."

They did, and Miranda dropped three nickels into the fare box. The trolley was almost full. "Emmy, you sit by the window," said Virginia, "and Miranda and I will sit behind you."

Emmy squeezed past a large lady with a basket of parcels next to her on the seat. As the trolley went on, she kept thinking about Pa walking away from her. She was sure it was him. Why didn't he come to give her a hug? Tears ran down her cheeks. She turned her face so that nobody would see and watched the blocks plod past.

The mules were as tired as she was. Once they stopped and wouldn't go again. The driver had to get out and talk to them and give each a carrot. Finally they leaned into their harnesses and walked on.

All the while, Emmy heard Virginia and Miranda behind her. They talked about the things Virginia had bought for Ma and Aunt Zena—the stockings and two sheets, four china soup bowls, and a needlework pattern. They talked until the driver said, "This's as far as I'm going tonight."

Miranda and the Fraileys were the last people off the trolley. They walked two long blocks home. Now nobody talked, but Miranda hugged Virginia and Emmy before she went into her house and said, "Thank you for taking me with you. I liked the stone hoist best of all."

When Miranda was safely out of hearing, Virginia said in a low voice to Emmy, "That *was* Pa we saw. He was with my ma's uncle Will."

Emmy started to cry again. "Why wouldn't you let me talk to him?"

"I couldn't let you say anything in front of Miranda, and we didn't know who else might be listening."

"Miranda wouldn't tell," said Emmy, sniffling.

"She might say something without thinking. Don't even tell my ma or yours. Just keep it to you and me."

Emmy saw Pa again that night, in a dream. This time he turned toward her and smiled.

9
STRANGERS IN THE HOUSE

Emmy never told anybody about seeing Pa. She kept a picture of him tucked away in her mind, where she could take it out and look at it before she fell asleep at night.

It was autumn now, and the summer heat had passed. The Frailey children had to wear shoes once again. Cool evening breezes swept down from the high mountains. The twins raked and burned heaps of dead stalks and leaves from the summer garden. Often thunderstorms crashed throughout the night. The earth smelled new in the early mornings when the twins and Emmy did the milking. Emmy loved the rich smells of burning, of damp dead leaves, of newly turned earth.

Friendship grew between Miranda's mother and Ma and Aunt Zena. Mrs. Champion often brought over her fine needlework and sat on the porch talking and rocking while the other women did their mending. Aunt Zena advised her to buy pinafores for Miranda to save her dresses. Ma told her which grocer carried the best butter.

By the time school began, Emmy and Miranda were almost as much twins, said Ma, as Ammon and Aaron. Together they scuffled to and from school through piles of fallen leaves. Mrs. Carter, the teacher, let them share a double desk.

Though Miranda was careful to stay out of the Frailey houses, she spent as much time as possible with Emmy. She learned the pull-and-squeeze for milking and the secrets of the egg-hiding chickens. If Emmy had to work in the garden, Miranda demanded a hoe or shovel to do her part. Together they shinnied up trees to pick apples and lugged bushels of potatoes into the root cellar for storage. After the burning summer, the cool air and scent of autumn filled them with bubbling energy.

Sometimes the girls begged permission to go down to the park, where the wide grassy fields gave them room to run. Sometimes they played paper dolls on the floor in Miranda's airy bedroom. They made a hideaway next to Coal Dust's stall in the Champions' barn.

On a dark cloudy afternoon in October, Ma asked them to go for lamp oil and salt at Brother Lichet's store, down two blocks and around the corner. Emmy kept her eyes open all the way. Several times she'd seen the shabby buggy of the bushy-bearded man Sam had talked to the day Pa went away. Some of the boys in the ward said that strangers had stopped to ask them news of this brother or that.

Miranda walked slowly, almost dragging her feet. On the way back she told Emmy, "My head aches. I think I'll go home and lie down." Her face was red and her brown eyes had no sparkle.

When Mrs. Champion saw Miranda, she took her straight upstairs and put her to bed. "She needs to sleep," she told the anxious Emmy. "She'll be all right tomorrow."

"Miranda's sick," Emmy told Ma when she gave her the oil and salt.

"I expect she'll be better in a few days," said Ma comfortingly. "We'll make her a custard."

As Emmy went to the outhouse before going to bed, she heard a rumble of thunder. The air was still and heavy. She hurried back inside and went upstairs to bed. But she found it hard to sleep as the thunder came nearer. A snap of lightning lit up her room, followed by a crack of thunder. Rain poured down. Emmy fell asleep to its steady beat.

In the middle of a tangled dream about Pa and Miranda driving away, a racket jerked her awake. It sounded like Pa hammering on the barn door to drive in loose nails. She sat straight up in bed. At first she thought it was more thunder.

And then she heard rough, angry voices.

Emmy got out of bed and felt her way through the dark

room to the doorway. She bumped into Ammon in the hall.

"What in tarnation was that?" asked Ammon just as the hammering began again.

"Somebody's knocking at the door," said Emmy, her insides churning.

They heard more shouting. "We'd best go down and see if Ma's all right," said Ammon.

Emmy's legs seemed to melt, yet she did not want to stay upstairs. She forced herself to follow Ammon down the stairs toward a glow of soft light.

Ma stood by the door with a candlestick. Her hair was braided down her back like Emmy's and she wore a shawl over her nightdress. As she turned the doorknob three men pushed inside.

They seemed to overflow the house with their thick boots and loud voices. "We're alooking for Malachi Frailey. This is his house, ain't it?" said one.

"My husband isn't here just now," said Ma calmly. Her candle flame trembled.

"Oh, he isn't! I think we'll just see for ourselves."

As the men shoved past Ma into the sitting room, Emmy's jelly legs gave way. Ammon and Ma sank down beside her on the bottom stair. They listened in silence to thumps, bangs, and terrible words that Emmy had never heard. She never wanted to hear them again.

Ma bent down and whispered, "Ammon, run tell the big boys. Tell them to hide, not to cause a ruckus. Emmy, go warn Aunt Zena. I'll be all right here."

Emmy's legs wouldn't work, until Ammon yanked her by

the hand. He dragged her through the hall and out the kitchen door. "Run!" he said.

She ran, stumbling and sobbing, through the streaming rain across the yards, cringing at every shadow. In Aunt Zena's dark kitchen somebody grasped her arm. "Who's there?" somebody whispered.

Emmy froze. Somebody scratched a match, lit a candle. "Emmy!" said Aunt Zena. "We heard a racket next door. What's happening?"

"Some men looking for Pa," said Emmy through chattering teeth. "Ma said to warn you."

"Calm down, child," said Aunt Zena. "Let them come. Pa isn't here. He's safe." Emmy saw Virginia and Aaron behind her, their faces white and frightened.

Aunt Zena said, "Emmy, you want to stay or go back with your ma?"

At the thought of the rough men in her house, Emmy's legs turned to jelly again. But she wanted Ma; she wanted to know if Ma was all right. Aaron went back with her. Light flickered wildly around the kitchen, so they went around to the open front door.

"You all right now?" whispered Aaron.

Emmy wasn't all right, but she nodded and he disappeared. As she crept down the hall toward the kitchen, a crash shook the house. "I'm here, Emmy," said Ma's quiet voice and Ma's arm reached out to encircle her. "That was just the table falling over."

From the kitchen doorway they watched one of the men climb down the steep cellar stairs. "That's food for our winter eating down-cellar," Ma called to him. "I'd be grateful if you did not destroy it."

When they didn't find Pa in the cellar, the men tromped upstairs. Ma and Emmy followed them into the boys' room. Sam, who had slept through all the noise, rubbed his eyes and blinked when he saw the strange men.

"What are they doing?" he said. "Oh, I know that man. And that one." Sam pointed to a thin man whose pants looked too big to stay up even with suspenders. And he pointed to the round-faced man with the bushy beard.

Mr. Bushy Beard looked startled. "All right, boys, let's not be so rough," he said. "There's a little'un here."

"Maybe the little'un knows where his pa is," said the thin man.

"My pa went away," said Sam. "He doesn't want to go to jail."

"I just bet he doesn't," said the thin man. He laughed and spat tobacco juice on the floor.

"My son doesn't know where his father is," Ma said, her voice shaking.

"Do you, lady?"

Ma sat on Sam's bed and held her son tightly. "No, I do not know where my husband is at this time, but I tell you truly, he is not on this property. I have not seen him for these past six weeks."

Mr. Bushy Beard looked down at the floor, as if he were ashamed. The thin man said, "All right, boys, let's try the other rooms and look around outside."

Ma and Sam and Emmy heard them stomp into Emmy's

tiny room and then into the attic where strips of apples and strings of green beans hung to dry. They clattered downstairs, banging the kitchen door on their way out.

The house was silent. Sam began to cry. "I don't like those men," he sobbed.

"It's all right, baby. It's all right. Ma's here, and Sister. We'll stay together. Emmy, you and Sam get under his quilt and get warm."

Ma tucked them in and sat on the end of the bed. Emmy wrapped her arms around her brother's warm little body. For a long time they listened. The rain wasn't as loud on the roof now. They heard no harsh voices, no more crashes. Emmy thought she heard horse hooves and wheels out on the street, but she wasn't sure. She didn't want to get out of bed to see if the deputies had left yet.

Ma began to sing in a quavery voice.

> Why should we mourn or think our lot is hard?
> 'Tis not so; all is right.
> Why should we think to earn a great reward
> If we now shun the fight?
> Gird up your loins; fresh courage take.
> Our God will never us forsake;
> And soon we'll have this tale to tell—
> All is well! All . . .

Ma stopped singing. "Listen," she said. Emmy heard it too. The stairs were creaking.

Somebody was coming upstairs.

10
FRIENDS IN NEED

Ma blew out the candle. Someone tip-toed into Emmy's room and out again. Slowly the boys' room door opened. A lantern appeared, turned low.

"Ma?" came a whisper.

"Gideon?" said Ma.

"It's Oliver. Are you all right?"

"Oh, Oliver!" cried Ma, and burst into tears.

Oliver shouted downstairs, "Come on up. They're all right." The rest of the family crowded into the boys' room—the four big boys and the twins, Virginia, and Aunt Zena. Ma and Aunt Zena hugged each other and wept. Sam and Emmy unsnarled themselves from Sam's quilt and sat up.

Everybody talked at once.

Oliver said, "We followed those men all over the place while they searched the outbuildings, and they never saw us."

Gideon laughed. "We dropped a pitchfork on the floor behind them when they went into the barn, and that spooked them. They seemed halfhearted-like, didn't you think, Ol?"

"Did they go to your place?" Ma asked Aunt Zena.

"Yes, but they didn't stay long." Aaron was anxious to tell his part of the story. "Somebody came to the door while they were messing around in the sitting room. They left pretty soon after that."

"They didn't do much to my place, Ellen," said Zena. "Pulled things off the beds. Poked around down in the cellar some, but they didn't smash anything."

Gideon and Oliver stayed in the house for the rest of the night. With so much family around, Emmy chose her own bed for sleep, but a long time passed before her eyes would close.

"Who hurt my house?" asked Sam when he came downstairs for breakfast the next morning. He had on his long nightshirt, and his hair stuck up like the rooster's comb. He looked at the scattered knives and spoons on the floor, at the smashed plate and upturned table.

Ma came up from the cellar, where she had been cleaning up a broken bottle of tomatoes. "Why, Sammy, our house isn't hurt. It's just untidy."

Emmy and the boys had just brought up the morning

milk; they reported that nothing was disturbed outside. Ma insisted that everyone eat before they started clearing up the mess from the last night's invasion.

They were just finishing their bread and milk when Miranda's parents came to the back door. Ma asked them in. This was not a day to worry about Pa and his distrust of all Gentiles.

"We're sorry about your trouble last night," said Mr. Champion.

"Now, how did you hear about that?" asked Ma.

"I saw an unfamiliar buggy outside your house as I drove home late last night," said Mr. Champion. "When I noticed lights moving around the other Sister Frailey's house, I decided to investigate. Three gentlemen came to the door in answer to my knock. I introduced myself as a reporter for the *Tribune*. But when I asked their names, they climbed into their buggy and skedaddled."

Mrs. Champion was staring at the kitchen. "Oh, my land," she murmured. "Why, you poor, poor woman."

"It isn't so bad," Ma said. "Mostly they threw things about. It's the flour all over the floor that makes such a mess. I can't imagine why they thought my husband was in the flour barrel."

"Is there anything we can do for you?" asked Mr. Champion.

"You chased those rascals away," said Ma. "That's what we needed most. How is Miranda? Is she feeling better?"

Mrs. Champion shook her head. "I'm keeping her in bed today. But her papa says she'll be fine soon."

* * *

Ammon and Emmy stayed home from school to help clean the house. In the sitting room the men had tossed books from their shelves, looking for a secret door. In the bedrooms they had dragged furniture around, torn a rag carpet, and pulled quilts and sheets off the beds.

The muddy marks of their boots were everywhere. Ma scrubbed at the floors as if they were covered with dirt deeper than mud.

Ma and Aunt Zena made some changes after the deputies came. They barred their doors each night, something they had never done before. The big boys moved back into their houses. Ma moved upstairs to sleep on a straw mattress in Emmy's room, and Gideon and Oliver slept downstairs.

Virginia began work as a clerk at the Z.C.M.I. in the housewares department. Every day she walked downtown early in the morning and back again after dark. She walked with two friends who had jobs in offices.

Ma and Aunt Zena decided that the whole family should eat dinner together each evening when the day's work was done. Emmy didn't mind setting the sitting-room table now. It was fun to have the big family gathered around the table. Virginia described the people who came into her department to buy pottery bowls and big wooden spoons. The big boys talked about their adventures delivering chairs.

Best of all, everybody cleaned up together. As soon as the meal was over, the big boys carried everything out to the kitchen. While the twins scraped plates into the pig bucket, Virginia filled the kitchen sink with hot water and soapsuds. Emmy stacked plates by the sink for Virginia to wash. Ma and Aunt Zena put away leftover food and set porridge to cook for the morning. Sam dried the knives and forks, and anybody not busy with something else dried plates and cups.

With everybody singing as they worked, the kitchen was soon clean. Last of all, Emmy and Sam set out knives and spoons for breakfast, covering each pair with an overturned plate to keep the dust off.

Emmy was grateful for the lively family evenings with their songs and games and chat. Her days stretched lonely and long, for Miranda was not getting any better.

Every day, when school let out, Emmy took schoolbooks and a slate over to the Champions' house to catch Miranda up with her schoolwork. At first Miranda eagerly practiced the twelve-times tables and listened to Emmy talk about Mrs. Carter's new roll-up map of the United States. But she tired soon, sometimes falling asleep before Emmy went home. After a while Mrs. Champion said Emmy had best not come in, Miranda was so tired all the time.

"Is she going to be all right?" Emmy asked.

Miranda's mother frowned a little. "Her papa insists she will be better soon. But I don't know. . . ."

After that, Emmy left some new thing each day at Miranda's house—a picture made out of dried leaves and flowers, a handkerchief with M.C. embroidered in one corner, a friendship ring braided out of her own hair. Each day Mrs. Champion said, "Thank you, Emmy. Miranda will enjoy this as soon as she is better."

One rainy October Monday, Mrs. Champion cried when

Emmy knocked on the door. "Miranda has typhoid," she said. "You mustn't come in."

Typhoid! Emmy ran straight home to ask Ma about it. Ma soothed her worries. "Many people have typhoid after a hot summer such as we've had, Emmy. I had it as a child."

"Don't people die of typhoid?"

"Some do," Ma admitted. "But Miranda is not a sickly child. She should be over it in a few weeks."

On Saturday the weather cleared after days of rain. A boisterous wind whisked clouds across the sky. Ma and Aunt Zena did laundry. They boiled all the sheets in the big tubs over the laundry-shed fire.

While the twins ran sheets through the wringer, the women washed underwear, shirts, and dresses, and finally the boys' pants and overalls in the last of the water. Emmy ran back and forth all morning between the laundry shed and clotheslines. She pegged out wet things, then took down damp things to iron and dry things to fold.

Near suppertime the clouds returned. Ma sent Emmy out to get the last of the laundry off the line. As she pulled the clothes-pegs off shirts and overalls, she watched the Champion house and wondered when Miranda would be able to play again. And then she noticed a horse and buggy tied down by the barn. It was Brother Brownard's—Doctor Brownard's. It had spent many hours outside the Champion house these past weeks.

Emmy dropped pegs and pillowcases into the laundry basket. She was over the fence and knocking at the Champions' kitchen door before she stopped to think.

Mr. Champion opened the door. "Come in, Emmy." His face drooped, as if he hadn't had much sleep. Mrs. Champion sat slumped on a kitchen chair in a crumpled dress. Her eyes burned out of the dark circles around them. Her hair was pinned up anyhow. She didn't look at all like the elegant woman Emmy had once feared.

Brother Brownard filled the doorway to the hall with his big bearlike frame and bushy beard. He set his battered instrument bag on the table and said, "I'll come back again later. She's a mighty sick little girl. Mighty sick."

Mrs. Champion began to cry. Emmy tried to swallow the lump that choked her throat. "But she's going to get better, isn't she?"

Brother Brownard stared at the floor. Mr. Champion pressed his head against the window and stared out into the dark evening. Miranda's mother put her hands over her face.

"You mean Miranda might *die*?" asked Emmy.

As he laid a hand on Mr. Champion's shoulder, Brother Brownard said, "Pray for her, Emmy. We will not lose hope."

Blindly Emmy stumbled out of the house and climbed the fence to her own yard. Miranda . . . die! Emmy couldn't see a stop to all the fun and life of Miranda. But if Brother Brownard couldn't make her better, who could?

Hardly knowing where she was going, she went past the clothesline and the barn to the pasture at the far end of the Frailey lots. Rust came over to the fence and she patted his nose, then pressed her face against his neck.

"Oh, Rust!" Somehow, somebody had to do something. She remembered Brother Brownard's words and began to pray. "Heavenly Father, take care of Miranda. . . ."

Suddenly she remembered Sam when he fell out of the tree at the picnic. She remembered him lying twisted and still on the ground until . . .

Until Pa gave him a blessing.

Pa! Pa needed to give Miranda a blessing.

But where was Pa?

Ma knew, she was sure. And so did Aunt Zena. But they would not tell Emmy.

Think! she told herself. There's something . . . something about . . .

Pa, that day down on Temple Square, with Virginia's great-uncle Will.

Emmy ran frantically up the path toward the houses. Virginia would know . . . but Virginia was still down at the Z.C.M.I. She would just have to make Ma tell her where Pa was hiding.

She almost smacked into the twins in her hurry. They were carrying pumpkins to the root cellar. "Where're you going so fast?" asked Ammon. "I thought you were doing laundry."

Emmy panted, "Aaron, where's your great-uncle Will live?"

The twins looked at each other and then back at Emmy. "Why?" asked Aaron.

"I need Pa." She saw in their eyes that they had known all along where Pa was. "He's at your uncle's place, isn't he? How did you know where he was?"

"Oh," said Aaron, "one night Ma and Aunt Ellen let fall something about Great-Uncle Will's farm down to the south."

"Pa took us there once when he went to repair Uncle Will's roof," added Ammon.

"Tell me how to get there," pleaded Emmy. "I need Pa, right away."

"Why?" Aaron asked again.

Hot tears ran down Emmy's face. "Miranda might die."

"Die?" asked Ammon. "How do you know?"

"Brother Brownard said she might. But if Pa could give Miranda a blessing like he did Sam, she'd be all right. I just know she would." Emmy pushed tears off her cheeks with her hands.

"Somebody else could give her a blessing. The big boys, maybe, or the bishop," suggested Ammon.

"It has to be Pa. *Please*, Aaron."

"We'll go get him for you," Aaron said.

"No, I need to go myself. Miranda is my friend."

"How are you going to get there?" asked Ammon. "Walk? It's miles down the valley."

"I'll ride Rust."

"What about Ma?"

"Say I'm at the other house. That's true; I'll be at Pa's house. But I've got to go *now*."

The twins exchanged another look. "It's cold," said Ammon. "She'd best wear my jacket."

Aaron nodded. "All right, Emmy. Here's how you go." He knelt down in the dust and began to draw a map. "Now you got to pay attention, see, so you don't get lost. . . ."

11
LOOKING FOR PA

It was a night of flying shadows. The wind kept blowing clouds across the moon and clearing them away again. There wasn't much traffic, only a wagon or two. As Rust trotted along, Emmy bounced on his slippery back, but she didn't want to slow him down. What if Miranda died because she took too long finding Pa? Whenever the half-moon showed the way, she kicked Rust into a lope.

Emmy rode past Liberty Park, where the houses weren't so close together. After a while the lighted windows of houses were even farther apart. She was out of the city now, riding past farms. The dark shapes of cows and horses came to fences to watch her pass. An occasional dog ran out to bark at Rust's hooves.

"Look for a crooked cottonwood tree," Aaron had said, "right in a fence corner, and turn toward the river." In the dark she didn't see the tree until she had almost gone past. She swerved Rust around the corner onto a road with deep wagon-wheel ruts and pulled him down to a walk.

Now she saw only shadowy tree branches swinging in the wind. She heard nothing but Rust's plodding hooves and an occasional snort.

Before long the road ended in a fenced field. Rust dropped his head to the ditch along the field and sucked in water. The twins had said nothing about a road ending in a field, she was sure. She went over their directions in her mind. Had she missed her way? She'd seen the dim bulk of a double barn on the right. Next there should have been a pine tree in a little cemetery. If she had gone wrong already, she didn't know how she could find Pa.

The wind blew the scattered clouds away from the half-moon as Emmy turned Rust. She let him walk, stopping when the moon disappeared. When its light returned, she saw the wind-bounced pine. She could even see two headstones. And there was the road.

Emmy rode along slowly, watching for the old log cabin Aaron said Great-Uncle Will lived in. She wound her fingers in Rust's mane, afraid she might fall asleep and slip off his back. Only the thought of Miranda kept her hanging on.

The cabin, when she finally found it, was completely dark. Emmy guided Rust into its farmyard. She couldn't seem to think what to do next. What if Pa wasn't here? What if he had to go hide somewhere else? What if this wasn't Great-Uncle Will's place, but a Gentile farm?

Suddenly a yapping dog rushed out and pranced around Rust's hooves. Startled, Rust jumped back and Emmy slid off. She landed on her feet, staggering to keep her balance. There was a low call from the shadows near the cabin. The dog disappeared.

Rust nudged her with his nose, snorting all over her. Emmy grabbed his reins to hold herself up. All she could think of was how to get back on Rust, how to find her way back home.

Suddenly a light flashed in her face. She closed her eyes and turned away from its unexpected brightness.

"Emma Leah!" It was Pa's voice!

"Pa?" whispered Emmy. "Pa, is that you?"

"Are you alone, Daughter?"

"Yes." She wanted to run to Pa, to hug him and tell him about Miranda, but Pa stayed in the shadows.

"How did you come here?"

"I rode Rust."

"Follow my lantern and bring him into the barn."

Emmy led Rust through the yard and into the dark barn. At last she saw Pa. He dragged the heavy door closed behind them.

He set his lantern down, then knelt down and put his arms around her and held her tight. When he pushed her back so he could see her, his face was wet. She saw that his beard had grown out, and his hair was almost to his shoulders.

Emmy began to cry too, she was so glad to see him.

"What's wrong, Emma Leah? Is your ma all right? And your Aunt Zena?"

"They're all right, Pa."

"And your sister and brothers?"

"All of us are all right. Truly, Pa."

He hugged her again. "Oh, I miss all of you so."

Emmy hugged him back tightly, safe in the circle of his strong arms, safe now in the light and out of the dark night.

But then Pa let her go. "How did you know where I was? How did you find me?"

Emmy told him about the twins and about getting lost.

Pa frowned. "Now, Emma Leah, why did you come?"

Tears filled Emmy's eyes and her throat tightened and became hot as she remembered why she had come. "Oh, Pa, it's Miranda. She's got the typhoid and Brother Brownard can't help her get better. I'm afraid she's going to die."

"The Gentile girl has the typhoid? What has that got to do with me, Daughter?"

Emmy took a deep breath before she spoke. "Remember how you said when we do all we can and we can't do any more, the Lord will help? Brother Brownard says he's doing all he can, but Miranda isn't getting better, Pa. I think she needs a blessing, like you gave Sam."

"Someone else could give her a blessing," said Pa, as the twins had said. "Gideon or Martin, perhaps."

"But I want you to, Pa. Please."

Pa rubbed at his mustache. "What about Miranda's father and mother?" he said. "What would they think if I walked into their house to say a prayer for their daughter? What do they say, eh? Did you ask them?"

"No, Pa," Emmy whispered. "I didn't think to ask them."

"Some Gentiles think we are heathens or devils."

"Mr. Champion isn't like that, Pa. He scared the deputies away." She told Pa all about that terrible night.

Pa hugged her tighter. "You've had quite a time," he said rubbing his mustache. "But what in tarnation made you come all this way, anyway, just to ask me to give a blessing?"

"You told me to be a faithful friend."

"I told you what?" asked Pa.

"The night you went away. You said, 'I bless you to be a faithful friend.' Can we go right now, Pa? Please?"

Pa stared down at the lantern. Then he said, "Let's give Rust here something to eat. We'll go rustle up food for ourselves and think this thing over."

Emmy clenched her teeth to keep from crying. She knew Pa couldn't be hurried. He had to think things through. Then he would do what he thought was best for everyone.

Pa lived in a room at the back of the barn. His lantern, hanging from a nail on the wall, showed a cot bed, a table and chair, a wood stove, a tin sink with a pump handle, and shelves on the wall above a small cupboard. Everything was neat and handy.

"I fitted it up myself," said Pa. He added wood to the stove. He opened the cupboard and brought out a bowl of eggs and another of boiled potatoes, which he set on the table. From the shelves he took a fry pan and a knife, plates, and forks. Emmy began to wonder if she were asleep and dreaming. Never had she seen Pa do any kind of kitchen work.

"I'll fry those potatoes, Pa," she said.

Pa silently handed her the knife and watched her slice potatoes into the fry pan on the stove.

"Your ma know where you are?" he asked suddenly.

"No, Pa, but the twins do."

"She's going to be mighty worried."

"Yes, Pa."

"You had any more trouble with those men who talked to Sam?"

"Yes, Pa. They were the deputies who searched our houses that night."

"Did they hurt any of you?"

"No," said Emmy. "They just made a terrible mess and went away."

"Have they been back since?"

"No."

"Have you seen anybody else you don't know?"

Emmy told him what the boys at school said about strangers driving up and down the ward streets.

Pa pulled at his mustache. He looked as weary as Emmy felt. She hefted the heavy fry pan from the stove to the table.

Pa served potatoes on a plate. "That enough for you?"

Emmy nodded, hoping she had enough energy to eat.

"I'll eat from the pan. It saves washing a plate."

This from Pa, who always wanted a properly set table in the sitting room, dishes and utensils arranged just so. He had changed during this time of hiding, living in this one room. Emmy ducked her head so Pa wouldn't see her cry, thinking about Pa living all alone.

"Let us pray," said Pa. Emmy folded her arms. Pa thanked the Lord for her safe journey and asked a blessing on the food. Then he added, "Bless the young Gentile girl, and show us the means of helping her, if it be thy will."

He ate hungrily. "You'll be a right smart cook someday. Now, you tidy up while I pack my things and tell Will I'm borrowing his wagon."

"Oh, Pa! Are you coming back home to live?"

"I can't, Daughter. They'd find me for sure."

For the first time, Emmy understood that, by asking Pa to come to Miranda, she was bringing him into danger. Pa . . . Miranda . . . how could she choose?

"Oh, Pa." This time Emmy did cry. "You stay here, Pa, where you're safe."

"I am not safe here any longer, Emma Leah. I knew the day I saw you down at the temple that I was foolish to stay so close to home."

"I knew it was you, Pa!" Emmy burst out.

"I felt I had to earn some money to send all of you," said Pa. "But I'd only been working three days when you saw me. It won't be long before someone else does too. If the twins could figure out this hiding place, so can others. It's time to move on."

Pa was silent for a few minutes, his head bowed. Then he straightened his back and nodded at Emmy. "You are right, Emma Leah. We are taught to love our enemies, after all. Let's go to your friend."

12
PA AND THE GENTILES

For the rest of her life Emmy often thought of that ride home under the blowing clouds. She and Pa sat side by side on the wagon seat, sharing a quilt to keep off the night chill and scattered rain. Her tiredness disappeared, though Pa would not hurry Rust and she knew it would be a long drive home. Never had she had Pa to herself for so long a time. Never had she felt so close to him.

He wanted to hear about each family member. She told him about Virginia's job, about school, about the hairy-legged spiders Sam liked to draw, about the family dinners.

"It hurts me to be away from you all," said Pa. "I pray for the time when we can live together again."

"When will that be, Pa?" asked Emmy.

"I don't know, Daughter. Nobody knows." Pa was silent for a long time before he went on. "If we cannot live here in peace, we will move south, maybe to Mexico."

Now it was Emmy's turn for silence. Other plural-marriage families were moving south. Might she have to leave her home and live somewhere new? Miranda had done so, when her family moved from Chicago to Salt Lake. But Emmy knew the choice would not be hers. Pa, Ma, and Aunt Zena would decide.

It was so late that they saw no lights anywhere, besides their own wagon lantern. The moon had gone down, and the wind had chased away the last of the clouds.

"Look up there," Pa said, tilting his head back to stare into the black star-speckled sky. "That's where we'll all live someday. Saints and Gentiles both. Maybe up there we can get along."

Near the park he called Rust to a stop. "Look around, Daughter. Hear anything? See anybody?"

Far away a dog barked. Everything else was quiet. As Pa chirruped to Rust and turned the corner to home, Emmy saw a light in the Champions' kitchen window. A bolt of panic licked through her. Were they too late?

Pa saw something else—another lantern on the street, several blocks away. "Emmy," he whispered, "I don't dare go home. Is there room for this wagon in the Champion barn?"

Emmy could see the lantern too, coming toward them.

"Yes," she whispered as her heart began to bang against her ribs, "it's plenty big."

Rust swung into the drive by the brick house and trotted back to the barn. As Pa pulled him to a stop, Emmy slid down from the wagon. She forced her shaking hands to find the latch and drag open the door. Pa drove quickly into the barn. Before she had the door quite shut he took her hand and they slipped outside, closing the door behind them.

A horse snorted, almost in Emmy's ear. She stumbled and almost fell, but Pa held her close.

"Hurry!" he said, half carrying her past a bulky shape to the shadow of the brick house. Through the apple trees they could see a lantern swinging down the drive between Ma's and Aunt Zena's houses, going toward the Frailey barn.

"Wait on Miranda's back porch," said Pa. And he was gone.

Emmy forced her legs up the porch steps. When she looked again, the lantern bobbing back up toward the Frailey houses had disappeared. In a few minutes she thought she heard the jingle of a harness, the muffled sound of hooves on damp dirt. Then nothing.

Now shadowy figures with a dim lantern came down the Champion drive. Emmy crouched in the darkest corner of the porch, trying to shrink herself out of sight. Her heart beat so frantically she thought the shadow people must have heard it.

Somebody raised the lantern high. Emmy stood up and,

by its light, saw what she had missed before—a horse and buggy, down by the watering trough.

Whoever held the lantern saw them too. Somebody called out, "It's the doctor's rig we saw, boys. No use looking around here any more tonight."

Emmy's head spun. Rust and Pa must be safe, she thought. But Miranda . . .

Suddenly Pa was back, though she hadn't heard or seen him move. "They've gone. We're all right. They won't search a Gentile house."

He tapped quietly on the kitchen door and Mr. Champion opened it almost immediately.

New lines dragged down his cheerful face. His eyes were red, but he held the door open for them. "Mr. Frailey, Miss Emmy. Please come in. I thought I heard a horse."

Pa and Emmy slipped inside and stood in a sheltered corner, well away from the kitchen's windows. Pa said, "We've left our horse and wagon in your barn, if that's all right."

"Of course," said Mr. Champion, pulling the curtains to shut out any view from the street. "You're welcome to spend the night, though I want to warn you there is typhoid in the house. My daughter . . . ," he said, in a trembling voice. "Doctor Brownard is upstairs with my wife."

"I'm sorry to hear that," said Pa. "Emma Leah thought perhaps I could be of use."

"We'd appreciate anything you can do," said Mr. Champion.

"Emma Leah," said Pa, "you explain."

Emmy took in a huge breath. She could still feel her heart banging. But now it was time to think about her friend. "I thought Pa could give Miranda a blessing," she said, "like he does to us when we're sick."

Mr. Champion nodded slowly. "A blessing."

"Yes," said Pa. "If Brother Brownard is in the house, he will lay his hands with mine on your daughter's head."

"I'm willing to try prayer. I'm sure my wife would agree. But are you sure you want to take the risk of infection?"

"I'll be all right," said Pa. "And Emma Leah will stay down here. Shall we go now?"

As the men went upstairs, Emmy sank onto a kitchen chair. She folded her arms on the table and laid her tired head down. Her heart began to slow down in the silent house.

She seemed to hear Ma singing the old Mormon hymn.

> And should we die before our journey's through,
> Happy day! All is well!
> We then are free from toil and sorrow, too;
> With the just we shall dwell! . . .

Emmy began to cry. Tears ran down her face, over her arms. Was Miranda's journey through? Would her beloved friend go up into those stars Pa had showed her? Would she truly be happy there?

Pa was going, and now Miranda. . . . They swirled together in her mind, round and round and out of sight. . . .

A voice spoke, very near. "Don't wake her. She can sleep on the sofa." She couldn't make herself climb out of heavy sleep into wakefulness and the pain of remembering.

Somebody was carrying her. Somebody was laying her down. She was warm. She was safe. She was asleep.

13
FAREWELL

She thought Ma was there, smoothing her head, calling her gently. "Wake up, Emmy. Come say goodbye to Pa."

Pa! With a jerk Emmy woke all the way up, blinking her eyes in the light from the lantern on the Champions' sitting-room table. Ma stood by the sofa where she had been sleeping under a warm afghan.

Emmy struggled to sit up. "Where's Pa?"

"He's outside, getting ready to leave."

"Where's he going?" asked Emmy, rubbing her eyes to shake the sleep out.

"He's going south, Emmy, to work in one of the new towns," Ma told her. "He'll stay with friends. Mr. Champion's going to drive him the first part of his journey. Then he'll take the train. Wrap my shawl around you; it's chilly."

"Miranda!" Emmy said, remembering last night. "What about Miranda?"

"She's asleep, dearie," Ma said. "Come to Pa now."

Outside, a faint gray lightened the black sky in the east. Pa stood with Mr. Champion and Brother Brownard near their buggies by the barn.

"I'll write in care of Mr. Champion, Ellen," said Pa. He kissed Ma, who tried to smile.

"Pa!" cried Emmy.

Pa put his arms around her. "I wouldn't forget my Emma Leah."

"You'll be so far away," said Emmy, hugging him close.

"Not for always, Daughter. And not for truly. We keep each other in our hearts."

Mr. Champion stepped up into his buggy. "It's getting light. We'd best go."

Emmy clung to her father. "Pa . . . what about Miranda?"

"The blessing Brother Brownard and I felt to give," said Pa, "promised a return to health. Is that not so?" he asked the doctor.

Brother Brownard nodded. "The little girl is resting well. We have every reason to hope she'll be up to mischief again in a few weeks."

"Brother Frailey . . . ," said Mr. Champion as Coal Dust took a few steps forward.

Pa looked him straight in the eye. "I am ready, Brother Champion," he said, and swung himself up.

Hand in hand, Ma and Emmy followed the black buggy down the drive and out onto the street. They watched it disappear around the corner.

"Pa's safe now, isn't he, Ma?" asked Emmy as they walked slowly back to their house.

"He's in good hands, dearie—the Lord's and Brother Champion's!" Ma gave Emmy a hug and went into the kitchen.

Emmy sat on her own back porch steps, still wrapped in the warmth of Ma's shawl and Pa's hug. She watched the pale sky erase the stars. Wispy clouds began to glow pink.

She heard Ma in the kitchen, singing hymns as always while she stirred the morning mush. She could see Aunt Zena bustling to and fro past her own kitchen window.

Gideon, Oliver, and Ammon clattered down the steps past Emmy on their way to barn chores. A few minutes later Aunt Zena's boys followed them. Virginia came out to the pump for a bucket of water. She waved at her sister.

Upstairs in the brick house, Miranda slept, getting better. Upstairs in Emmy's own house, Sam sprawled out safely in his little bed.

Warm peace filled Emmy's heart as she heard Ma sing:

> But if our lives are spared again
> To see the Saints their rest obtain,
> Oh, how we'll make this chorus swell . . .

And Emmy joined in:

> All is well! All is well!

*A*FTERWORD

The song that Emmy and Ma sang, "Come, Come, Ye Saints," is still a favorite hymn of Latter-day Saints. Their church is divided into geographical units called wards, which are like the parishes of other churches.

The Church of Jesus Christ of Latter-day Saints, also called the Mormon Church, began in 1830 in New York State. Mormon elders traveled around the country preaching their gospel. Many people joined the new church and came to live with the other Saints.

As the church grew during the next sixteen years, the Saints moved several times. Each time they settled into a new area, there were problems. Some people who already lived in those places resented so many new people moving in. They feared that the Mormons would have too much political power.

They also did not agree with some Mormon beliefs. For example, the Saints did not practice slavery, which angered slave owners in Missouri. Mormons also believed that God wanted some of the men of their church to build up a righteous generation and have many children by having more than one wife at a time. This kind of marriage is called plural marriage, or polygamy.

Most non-Mormons believed that polygamy was wrong and immoral. In the traditions of the Jewish faith and of non-Mormon Christian religions, each man had only one wife. Only if his wife died or if they were divorced could he take another wife.

The Saints saw themselves as a people chosen by God. Some of them insisted that God gave them the land where they were settling. They often used the term *Gentile* for everybody who was not Mormon. These things irritated many non-Mormons.

Such disagreements often led to violence. The Mormons were driven out of one place after another. Some Mormons fought back, which didn't help.

The Saints looked for a place where they could live in peace according to their religious beliefs. In 1847 they began to move into the Utah Territory, to a wide grassy valley near a huge salty lake. They thought nobody else would want to live in this uninhabited area.

But soon hundreds of people poured through Salt Lake Valley on their way to search for gold in California. Some Gentiles decided to stay in the valley. At the same time, more and more Mormon converts moved to Utah. The old problems started again.

In 1852 the Church publicly announced the teaching of plural marriage. Church authorities asked many Mormon men to take more wives. Polygamists believed they were doing what God had asked them to do. Nobody knows how many of the Mormon men became polygamists. A good guess is about one-tenth of them.

Mormon women chose to marry men who already had at least one wife for all kinds of reasons. Some women—or their families—believed it was better to marry a faithful Latter-day Saint polygamist than a single Mormon man who did not live his religion. Some fell in love with a polygamist. Some women, who believed that they should marry for religious reasons, had no one else to marry. Some widows, like Ma, wanted to be part of a good Mormon family. Families and family life have always been an important part of the Latter-day Saint religion.

In the nineteenth century, it was difficult for unmarried women to earn a living. Being married meant being secure. Still, not every Latter-day Saint woman married. Mormon leaders encouraged women to get an education, partly so they could care for themselves when necessary.

Polygamy wasn't an easy way of life. Some polygamous families got along well and some did not, just like other families. In some families, all the wives and children lived in the same house. In others, each wife had her own house for herself and her children.

Meanwhile, the United States wondered what to do with Utah Territory. Should Utah be made a state? The Latter-day Saints wanted statehood for Utah. From 1849 on, the Saints asked to have their territory made into a state. They felt they would have a better chance to govern themselves as a state than as a territory. The laws for territories were made by the federal government of the United States.

The Saints were united in their political opinions and votes. They chose strong Latter-day Saint members to run for public office. They also gave women the right to vote. The Gentiles in Utah did not all think and vote alike, so the Saints won most elections. Not many Gentiles had a chance to hold political office in Utah Territory.

Many Gentiles wanted to keep a territorial government, in which the United States government appointed people to political offices. With a territorial government, Gentiles had a chance for political power in Utah.

The Mormon religion and way of life, especially polygamy, became an important part of the question of statehood for Utah. Congress began to make antipolygamy laws. In 1882, one such law made polygamy a crime. Any man found guilty of living with more than one wife was fined or even sent to jail. Some of these laws were made only for territories, like Utah, not for the rest of the United States.

To enforce the new laws, the government hired lawmen who earned a reward for every polygamist they turned over to government authorities. Some of these deputies wanted to make a lot of money and didn't care what they did to find polygamists. They frightened children by asking about their families and broke into houses at night to search for the wanted men.

The Saints argued that the antipolygamy laws took away their religious freedom and were therefore unconstitutional. They were required, they said, to obey God's commandments. To live their beliefs, many Mormon men spent months in jail or hiding "on the underground," separated from their wives and children.

Plural families had a hard time caring for themselves without their husbands and fathers. Some men chose, like Emmy's Pa, to move with their families to Mexico or Canada, where they could live in peace according to their beliefs about marriage.

In 1887 a new antipolygamy law was passed that meant church property was taken away because the church taught polygamy. People who believed in plural marriage could no longer vote or hold a public office.

In 1890 the church leaders, after much prayer, agreed to stop plural marriages. Gradually the men came out of jail and out of hiding. Some men settled down with just one of their families, leaving their other wives and children to live without a husband or father. Other men went to Canada or Mexico. Still others quietly went on living as they had before. Since that time, the church has not permitted plural marriages.

Utah finally became a state in 1896.

Would I like to share my husband with another wife? I

don't think I would! But I'm grateful that some early Saints chose to live in polygamy. If they hadn't, I, like Emmy, wouldn't be here!

KRISTIN EMBRY LITCHMAN
March 1997

Come, Come, Ye Saints

Text: William Clayton, 1814-1879
Music: English folk song

Doctrine and Covenants 61:36-39
Doctrine and Covenants 59:1-4

*A*CKNOWLEDGMENTS

Special thanks to Jessie L. Embry, assistant director of the Charles Redd Center for Western Studies at Brigham Young University, for her help in verifying the historical accuracy of this story.

ABOUT THE AUTHOR

KRISTIN EMBRY LITCHMAN lives in Albuquerque, New Mexico, with her husband. They have two grown daughters and six grandchildren. A descendent of Mormon pioneers, she grew up in Los Alamos, New Mexico, and is a graduate of the University of Utah.

She and her husband enjoy folk, contra, square, and English country dancing and teach traditional dance in the United States and Europe.

All Is Well is her first novel for Delacorte Press.